MILO

XAVIER'S HATCHLINGS BOOK 3

KATHI S. BARTON

This is a work of fiction. Names, characters, places, and incidents are products of the author's imagination or are used fictitiously and are not to be construed as real. Any resemblance to actual events, locations, organizations, or persons, living or dead, is entirely coincidental.

World Castle Publishing, LLC
Pensacola, Florida
Copyright © Kathi S. Barton 2021
Paperback ISBN: 9781955086387
eBook ISBN: 9781955086394
First Edition World Castle Publishing, LLC, June 28, 2021
http://www.worldcastlepublishing.com
Licensing Notes
Cover: Karen Fuller
Editor: Maxine Bringenberg

Prologue

Long ago, at a time when all creatures roamed the earth as only their true self. Working with and helping humans in whatever way they could. Where magic was celebrated. And dragons darkened the skies every day. It was then man figured out there was magic in the dragons and hunted them to almost extinction.

"I'm afraid there is no hope for us." No one made a sound as their leader continued. "Once the humans found out about us and what we can do for them dead, we were doomed. I'm so terribly sorry."

Coop looked around the room. There were so few of them now he could easily count them. When he had been younger, thousands of years ago, there would not be enough room for all of them to share this room. Now they were down to having a quarter of them share the space because so many, his own wife included, had been murdered so needlessly. Coop was saddened by it all. Turning to leave the large cave, he was stopped by his brother, Xavier.

"The boys, they are well?" He nodded and smiled. Coop felt it all the way to his heart, a place that had been dead for so long, it seemed. "You have the spell? You are going to use it on them? I so wish I had thought of this before my own family was taken from me, Coop. You are a brave man and a good father."

"Thank you. And I shall use it tonight. It is the only way to save them." Xavier nodded, his own heart heavy with the losses they had suffered. "You know I would have shared should I have had it sooner. I am so sorry, brother. All of my heart, it's sorry for you."

"I know that. I do. But they are all gone now. My other half, my children. Killed for things not fair to our kind." Coop knew all too well. "Aria was a good woman, Coop. A good woman and mother to your sons. She will be missed forever."

"Aye, in my heart and those of my sons." Xavier stood there for several seconds, and Coop told him he must go. "They're awaiting word on what is to happen with us all."

"One more thing, if you please. It will not take but a second. I have left them all I have. It is where you keep them hidden away, the boys. Deep within the cave, it's all there." Coop asked him what he meant. "I cannot go on, brother. I cannot. There is too much grief in my heart for me to live. I have left my things for them there. They might survive this, with the magic you have to give to them. And if so, they'll need more than you have to help them."

"Xavier, please, you mustn't do this. They'll miss you as much as I." Xavier nodded and said it had begun. "You can come and stay with my sons. You'll live with them in the caves, and they'll care for you."

"Nay. I cannot. I must go. Just tell them I love them. With all of my heart." There would be no stopping him once his heart was made up, Coop knew this, but it made his heart no less full for it. "Goodbye, my brother. Take care you are not caught by the humans."

Coop made his way back to his hidden cave and sat before the fire. The boys, he knew, were resting, their bodies getting stronger daily with their age. Soon they would be as big as him, dragons of worth and size. When his eldest son came to him, his eyes full of fear, Coop knew it was well past time he did what he had been practicing. The magic would keep them safe.

Gathering his sons, six of them of varying shades of blues and greens, he asked them to have a seat. He had a story to tell them. It was not a story, not truly, but a tale that would, hopefully, keep them safe.

"A witch told me once of a great magic only few can do. It takes a loving heart and a strong dragon to make it work. I have asked her, and she has told me how to make it so. In this magic, it will keep you all safe from the humans." They nodded, each of them knowing it was a human blade that took the life of their dear mother. "I will perform this upon you, each of you at the same time, and give you some magic you will use when you need it. This magic, strong and powerful, will let you roam with the humans, and they'll not know your true self is just below your flesh."

"You mean we'll be humans as well?" He nodded, then shook his head at Cooper, his oldest. "I don't understand, Father. Will you explain?"

"Yes. The magic I will give you will let you change into your true self when you are alone. But when you are out in the world, you will need to be a human. A man." Cooper looked at his brothers, then back at him as he continued. "With this magic, I will also give you a gift. Something you will need to keep yourself safe should they find out. A stronger armor than any other dragon before you, as well as the same immortality you have now, as man or dragon."

Hudson stared at him for long moments. He was the thinker, and if he could think of a reason for this not to work, he would voice it loudly. He was much like his mother in that. She would be the first to say when she did or did not like something. And the first to say the plan was perfect. He only hoped she would have approved of this.

"I think you are very smart, Father, to try and keep us safe. But I can only think this will not work on you. Or is that your plan?" The boy was much too smart, Coop thought. "If you change us, who will change you?"

"There will be no one to change me, son. I will.... It is my wish to join your mother in this earth." He watched them, seeing if they understood the love he had lost when she was murdered. "Giving you this magic, it will be something I can tell her I've done for her sons. You know as well as I that she loved you more than anything on this earth, including herself."

"She died saving us." Coop nodded at Lincoln. "I'm not happy you're going to die, Father, but I understand wanting to be with Mother. I miss her more every day."

"As do I." He looked at his sons, all of them growing into dragons of worth. "I must have an agreement from you all. Even if one of you does not want this, it will not work. I would say you should think on this hard. For once I have given this to you, there will be no going back."

"I wish to have it." He knew Cooper would be the first. Not that he did not love his father, but

Cooper would see things in a way most would not. To not have this done would mean a certain death for them all. Dragons were too valuable dead not to be hunted for all time. "I will do whatever it takes to make sure you are proud of me as well."

"I am already, Cooper. Forever."

The others nodded too. They were ready for this as much as he was dreading it. Because once he started the process to change his sons into men, he would begin to die. It would take all he was to change them.

Standing up, spreading his wings out behind him, Coop told them about the things their uncle had left them. They knew where the family jewels were, the things their mother had left them as well. Once they were standing, their bodies strong and healthy, he felt his heart swell and break for what he was about to do.

"I, Cooper Manning, of the Manning Dragons of the earth, give to my sons, Cooper, Hudson, Lincoln, Lucas, Tristan, and Xavier, all I am. Each of you will take a part of the earth with you when you are converted. The part of you that is unique in all ways will be strengthened and enhanced. You will be immortal, forever, and those you take to your hearts will be as well." His sons bowed before him when he told them to. He said the words over them that would change them to men. Coop could feel his body shutting down, his heart beating a little less. But he had one more thing he wished to bless them with and held himself upright to give it from his own dying heart. "One day, true love will come to you. And you will have more than you have ever known. It will fill you in ways you cannot ever imagine. Love will be yours for all times. For only then will you become a true dragon, a Manning Dragon."

~*~

Cooper sat with his brothers while their father lay dying. His heart was weak from what he had done, and it was tearing him apart. Father was weak, yes, but he continued to tell them tales of their mother, of their adventures when they were only small dragons. They were going to be alone soon; their father was so close to joining their mother it hurt Cooper in ways he had not expected.

"What shall we do with his body?" Cooper looked at Tristan and asked him what he meant. "He will not be able to lie here. If the humans were to find him, they would surely cut him up into pieces. I do not want that for him. We were never able to bury Mother in the proper way after what they did to her."

"We could burn his body." Cooper wondered how it would work when Hudson continued. "His scales will be worthless to them should they come upon his body. The magic he held within him also will be useless to them. He will be nothing more than a carcass. They'll leave alone."

Burn his body. It was something to think about. But he did not want to, not while he was still breathing, his body still alive. When he laid his head upon his father's chest, hearing his heart beating slower and slower, Cooper wondered what his father would think if he knew the magic he had given them had not worked. They were all still as dragons.

"He gave his life to keep us safe. But it did not work." No one said anything to him as they each watched their father. "Dragons such as we are, we'll be hunted and killed by the humans. There is nothing we can do but wait for them."

"We will survive if we stay here." Cooper told Xavier they would have to leave eventually. "To feed and to fly, yes. But perhaps we could do it only at night. To keep to the skies and not let them see us."

"They know we are about and will have spies out looking for our lairs. We will have to kill any man should he come for us, and still, we will not be safe. We are, after all, dragons who have a great deal of magic."

Cooper stopped breathing. Cooper did not hear his father's heart and knew it was at an end. He was quiet for a bit longer, waiting, hoping for just one more beat, one more sound that would mean he was still alive. But there was nothing. Their father was dead. Sitting up, he told them he had passed from this world into the next.

None of them had ever seen a dragon die before. Their mother had been dead when they found her. Each dragon they had come upon when they were out had been dead long before they found them, their bodies stripped of every part, so they resembled less of a dragon than just a pile of bones.

Their scales were used for roofs for their homes and for shields. The very meat of them was roasted and stored away so it could be used for medicines and potions. Hearts were cut up and dried, then ground into a powder to use for other things the humans would use to keep them from sickness, as well as magic to have a grand garden and trees heavy with fruit. The only part that would be left was the bones, and sometimes even those were carried off and used for something. Cooper hated all humans.

"We will do as suggested by Hudson. It is the only assured way we can—"

Before he could finish, he felt the stirring of the earth. It shook so hard it knocked each of them off their feet. As they lay there, terrified someone was coming for them, their father appeared before them.

His body was still aground. But instead of dark in death, he was brilliant in light. Faeries, thousands upon thousands of faeries, seemed to be covering him. Before Cooper could tell them to stop, to leave him alone, Father spoke.

"I love you, my sons." Each of them nodded, fear almost something he could touch. "I will now and forever join my true love, your mother. I must warn you, when you find your other half, and you will, you will have to be careful of the slayers. They will know what you have found by the magic you both will share. My sons, you will leave this place and take your place among men. Becoming someone I will be proud of."

"Father, the magic didn't work. We're still dragons." Cooper felt shameful to say a thing like that to his father. To tell him his sacrifice had not worked. "We will be hunted and killed."

"Nay, you only need to think of being your other half. Becoming a man is simple. The same when you wish to be your true self." Cooper was not sure what that meant, but his father continued before he could ask. "Go now, before men come here. The magic to hide me will draw them here. Be safe, my sons, and know I love you more than I do any other creature on this place."

Cooper stood then, the faeries still working, taking the body of his father apart. But as he watched, he could see they were not doing anything but preserving his body. Faerie ropes were all around him, and strings of magic were wrapped around him like a cocoon. It made him invisible to all. As Cooper stood there, his brothers beside him, he knew that, like him, they mourned the loss of yet another parent.

"You are the eldest." He nodded to the faerie when she asked. "We have a gift for you. For all of you, but you will receive the most. Your father was a great man, your mother a queen among her people. We wish to bestow upon you all your father had."

"My brothers, they will need it as well. I should like to share." She smiled at him and bowed. "What have you done with his body?"

"He is being prepared to be moved. We will make a grand garden upon him. Flowers will be there for all to see, but only a few will know a dragon is there with his other half, his love." He nodded. It was as it should be. "You will take this gift? You will share, but as I said, you will get more than the others."

"I don't care. Please, just do what you must so we can hide." She nodded again and touched her fingers, small, tiny ones, to his forehead. Then she did the same to the others before coming back to him. "It is done. You have shared it with us?"

"I have, Lord Cooper. But you must leave here now. There are humans coming. The magic we used to do this thing has given them cause to come here." He nodded and looked at the ground where their father had been. "He is safe. Just as your mother is now. Go before they find you here and murder you as well."

He thanked her for her help and left. The exit from this part of the cave was hidden so well only they knew about it. As they made their way into the night, he thought of the human inside of him, and the pain of it took his breath away. In seconds, he was down on his knees. Whatever was happening, he was surely going to die.

"You're a man." He looked up at his brothers as they began to transfer to men themselves. "We'll be safe now, all of us. We'll be humans for them until we can find a place where we can be ourselves."

"I don't think that's ever going to happen again." Hudson nodded and held his head tightly as he did so. "We will need to train ourselves in their ways. Become what they are. But never monsters."

"No, never." They made their way to a building; any would do for now. Hudson, like him, was staggering a little, but they were getting stronger as they moved. He turned to look at him as they were settling in the empty shell of a house. "We will need to buy things, houses and such."

"Yes. But tomorrow. I am too tired to think beyond how much we have lost." Hudson and the others agreed. "When the humans are gone from our cave, we'll go and find what Father was telling us about earlier, about the wealth that will keep us safe."

"I only hope there is a great deal of it. I don't know how to work, much less walk around like they do." Cooper told Xavier, the youngest brother, they would soon learn. "I hope so. I hope so."

He did as well. It was going to be hard enough for them to learn to eat and dress like humans, much less get around. Cooper hoped this worked. For he was as afraid as he had ever been in his life.

~*~

After a time, thousands of years, each of the dragons turned into men, forging their way into a world that was so different than the one they had been born to. It seemed a different planet. But survive they did.

Having their mates come to them, children born to all of them, gave them hope. A small and fragile thing after such hardships they were born to. Cooper became, as his father had been before him, the king of dragons—his mate, Carson, their queen. It had been and still was a time for celebration. To this day, they commemorated often and hard at each new birth of the dragons turned men and women.

The others, his brothers, prospered too, finding their other halves, making their magic stronger for having their love. They worked hard in keeping everyone safe and well fed, humans or other dragons. No one, not anyone in need, would have ever been turned away from their help. The Manning Dragons, true to their father and mother, became the most powerful dragons ever born.

Of the six sons, Xavier's sons, four hatchlings, and two humans moved far away to be the next generation of Manning dragons who would open their hearts and doors for all creatures. Even the sons of their heart, the two human-born men, carried powerful magic. They used it, with their brothers, to help as many creatures as possible, humans and dragons alike, to live in the ever-changing world. To help them not only succeed but to perhaps help someone else when they needed it. These boys, now men, have stories to tell.

Chapter 1

George and Theo were at the airport when the plane landed. They'd gotten breakfast together, then had gone to a craft store to pick up some things to make some embarrassing signs to welcome their brother home. Sure, he'd only been gone for a few days, but the three of them were closer than the rest of them. As soon as Theo saw his brother, the signs were discarded, and he and George rushed to their brother.

"What's happened?" Milo told them to just get him home. "Sure. But you're going to tell us why you look as if you've lost everything. Did someone hurt you, Milo? Where are they? Are they still here at the airport?"

Theo was looking around and missed that his brother had stopped moving. Going back to him, he told him he was sorry. George was asking him again what they needed to help him with. Milo said he just wanted to go home. That he was exhausted.

He must have been. No sooner had they gotten his luggage from the jet and Milo into the car than he was sound asleep. They'd planned to spend the day with him, getting lunch with him and hooking up sometime during the day with Jamie in order to see if the two of them were mates. But this seemed serious enough that Theo debated telling his mom.

I know he's tired. Theo hadn't been so relieved to hear his mom's voice as he was in that second. *I spoke to him on the plane. The poor boy has been working double shifts for us in getting some information, and he's worn out. Nothing more, just exhausted.*

I've never seen him like this before. For that matter, anyone. She said she'd told him to rest up, but he was stubborn. *Yes. I wonder who he might have gotten that from?*

Not me. Theo laughed and told George what Mom had said. He thought that Milo was stubborn, but Mom was ten times worse. *Anyway. If you're finished insulting your mother, I'd like for you to get him home and into his bed. Anything you were planning with him can wait until he can enjoy it more. Also, it might be a good time to take Jamie over to see him. While he's out. It might be sneaky, but you'd have an answer. I want one, too, as a matter of fact.*

He didn't feel good about that, but his mom

was right. They'd all know and could move on to the next phase, whatever that would be. Theo did think that Milo could use a mate, if for no other reason than for him to get laid. Also, she'd be there to make sure he didn't overwork himself like Milo tended to do.

Stopping by Jamie's house seemed to be the best course of action. While he didn't want to wake Milo to have him sniff her, George had pointed out that if she were his mate, she could take him into her home instead of them taking him across town to his own. Where someone would have to be there all the time.

"I can tell you don't have a mate." George asked him what that was supposed to mean. "You wouldn't dream of saying something that selfish to your own mate."

"What the hell does that mean?" Theo told him. "Oh. Well, I suppose I was being selfish, and it was a little sexist of me to want to pawn our brother off on a woman. I didn't think of it as it being her duty, but I did want to have him well cared for. I guess I need to work on that, being a better male when it comes to what I think a woman should be doing."

"You don't have to if you want to have the shit knocked out of you by your mate." George asked him if he thought his mate would be a ball cruncher. "Have you met any of the Manning women, George? I mean, there isn't a timid one in the bunch. That goes for our mates too. I'd not want to take on any of them. And work very hard in keeping on their good side. Related or not, I think they'd find a way to have me fall from a great height and let me lay there until I healed."

They pulled into the driveway of Jamie's home. It was something, this home that she'd just had updated. It was larger than his by a great deal, and even Finn's home was small by comparison. She was sitting on the front porch, rocking in what appeared to be like one of the swings his parents had at their home when he'd been younger.

"I think I might have run off Jangles. He was here for a little while this morning but decided I'm going to have to find me something to do." Jamie laughed. "I've been getting my recertification to work in the new hospital. What are you guys up to?"

"We've brought Milo over to see if he's your mate." Theo looked at George and wondered if the guy would ever find a way to ease into a conversation. He was entirely too blunt and honest right from the start. "Mom said you might be able to tell, and then we'd all know."

"You're not getting on my good side, George." He asked her why not. "Because this isn't how I wanted to start my day off. I was going to take a walk. Then maybe go into town and have some lunch. I don't think I've ever eaten a meal out on my own before. Now you two show up with my potential mate and fucking ruin my day."

"I'm sorry, Jamie." She looked over at Theo as he told George to get back in his car. "I don't know what we were thinking. Milo is going to rest up for a little while, and he'll see you when he sees you. I'm sorry."

"How does this work?" Theo asked her if she wanted to see too. "I do. I don't know what it might mean for me, or him for that matter, but I'd like to know. Since you're here already. Will he wake up if I'm his mate?"

"Honestly? I haven't any idea. Mom didn't give us any details when we spoke to her about it. She just said to come by and see if you might be his mate. You don't have to do this." She told him she knew that. "All right. I guess you'd have to do the sniffing thing. I know you hate that, but I really don't have any other idea on how we need to check."

Leaning into the back seat where Milo was sleeping, she stood up. The look on her face was pure confusion. When she didn't say anything, he didn't either. However, George didn't have the filter that he would hopefully get when he found his own mate.

"Are you?" She looked at his brother, then looked at him. "You're teasing us, aren't you? That's good that you can have a sense of humor about this. I know that when my mate comes along, I'm going to dazzle her—"

"Hush." George snapped his mouth closed with an audible click. Jamie looked at Theo before she spoke again. "He smells funny. I don't know what it is, but it's like he's ill. I haven't any idea why, but he smells of old blood."

"Old blood or iron?" She asked if there was a difference in the smells. "I don't know the answer to that, but Milo isn't a dragon. I didn't think iron would kill him any more than it would any of us, but if you smell it, that's something we need to have checked out. I'm going to call Winnie here. She's the protector, and she might be able to help with what it is you're detecting on him."

Winnie appeared just as he finished telling her what was going on. She asked him a couple of questions that he didn't know the answer to. He and George were told to take Milo into the house, and Theo was surprised when Jamie was all right with that. She enjoyed her alone time more than any person he knew.

"I smell iron too. Not a great deal of it, but he's sick with it. I doubt that he'd die from it, but it has affected him." She put her hand on his belly then up around his chest. "It's here. Surrounding his heart. After I take it out, I'm going to leave here to make sure I find the person responsible for this. All right? That means you'll have to wait for questions from me. If you have any, now would be the time to tell me."

"Is he my mate?" Theo watched Winnie as she seemed to struggle with answering Jamie. "I mean, all I could smell on him was the iron, as it turns out. If you can figure that out, I'd like to be made aware of it now."

"Much like you, I can't focus on anything but his illness. Trust me when I tell you, it will become clearer in the days ahead. Can he stay here? His faerie will be with him. If it's too much of a burden for you—"

"No. I want him to stay here. For no other reason than that, I owe this family my life, and I will do anything needed of me to take care of one of their own." Winnie nodded, then asked if she had any more questions. "Just one more. No biggie, but if he is my mate, will I have to worry about iron too?"

"Yes."

Winnie turned back to Milo. The bed he was lying on was perfect for his size. Whoever made the bedroom suite for this room had kept in mind that all of the Mannings were larger than life. Milo was the shortest at six foot ten inches.

Winnie didn't strain or anything like that when the iron that had been in his brother's body was pulled free. As soon as she put Milo into a deeper sleep, she told them, she disappeared, taking what appeared to be about a cup of iron in small, almost powered particles. Lily, Milo's faerie, knocked at the window, and it was Jamie that let her in.

"Whatever you need, you tell me, and I'll make sure you have it." Lily told her thanks and went to her master. "I'm assuming he's going to sleep for a little while. I'll be around if you need me."

Jamie just left them there. Theo looked at his brother, then at George. Neither of them seemed to understand what had just happened. Was she mad at them? Did she not want him in her house now?

Instead of standing around without answers, Theo went to find her. She was the closest thing he'd had to a sister, excluding Rachel, and he didn't want her upset with them. He found her in the kitchen.

"I'm going to have some cookies and tea. Would you like some?" He told her that would be good. "I'm going to talk, but so you know, I don't want you to answer. I'm just babbling right now, and if I don't, my head is going to explode. All right?"

"Yes. However, if I can answer, do you want me to?" She shook her head as she put a kettle on the burner to make some tea. "You do need to sit down, Jamie. I can hear your heart beating very quickly, and I don't want you stressed out. Just have a seat, and I'll make us the tea while you babble."

She sat down but played with the cup and saucer she'd been holding. He pulled the kettle off the burner then put his hand on it. In a shorter time than it would have taken the stove, he had hot water.

Pouring them both a cup and finding her stash of scones, he sat down across from her. She stared at him for several moments before she spoke.

"I'm not going to lie to you when I tell you I'm terrified of becoming a mate to any of you." He asked her why. "I've come from a long line of people with mental illness. When I went to visit Missy yesterday, the doctor told me her illness is hereditary. It's like a missing gene, he told me. That it more than likely would make it so that if I were to have two children, one of them would be affected by it."

"No, not anymore." She looked at him instead of at her teacup then. There was so much hope on her face that he was really glad he could help her out with this. "You're not able to have any illnesses. That would include anything that might well have been passed down to you. The reason I know this is because when I was younger, I asked one of my aunts if the possibility of having gene pool issues would be a problem for an animal as big as we are. As in, what if a mate was ill with something like you're talking about, how would it affect a dragon. She told me it wouldn't be there. That essentially, when you were given the ability to live forever, you'd be free of anything like that, along with cancer and other long-term illnesses. You'd have nothing in your DNA that would produce a child with a handicap."

"Will you and Pem have children?" He told

her they were working on figuring that out. "Because you're a dragon, and she's not. I would imagine that her having an egg would be difficult since she isn't built for that."

"My brothers and I are the first generation of dragons that were born to dragons that were turned into human shifters." He explained to her that his father was a dragon when he'd been born and changed to shift into a human when he was just a young dragon. "So, in answer to your question, I don't know if we'll be able to have any. You and Milo would be able to if he's your mate. You're neither one dragons, so we're betting that the possibility of you having a child would be better than with me having one with Pem."

"Because of the dragon thing." He laughed and told her that was it. "I don't know if I'm his mate. I don't know what to think about him being the one either. I'm just getting my life together and figuring out what I can do. I'm not saying that I'd turn him down. I mean, just hanging around you guys, I know there isn't anyone better than the Manning men."

"Thank you for that. I'll pass that on to my parents. They'll be happy to know they did a good job of raising us." Theo sipped his tea. He didn't push her into whatever else she wanted to talk about but let her work it out. Looking around the kitchen, he realized that she was doing for herself. There was no cook here. No staff that he'd come across. He wondered if she had not hired them because of her need to have things quiet or just hadn't gotten around to it. Theo started to ask her about it when she spoke again.

"I've noticed that you don't tell Pem what to do. Do you suppose that if Milo is my mate, he'll do the same thing?" Theo told her he thought she could put him in his place if he did start that. "Yes, I suppose I would. I'm not much of a people person. I'm all right once I get to know you, but I'm not the sort of person that goes out much and parties. I prefer a good book over the television. Working in the yard instead of being in the house. Also, I enjoy just being out of doors. I'm not sure how that is going to work either."

"It'll work because the fates have chosen you if you are above all other women in the world to match up perfectly with your mate. Milo, for the most part, would rather stay home than to date. All of us enjoy the outdoors. I think a lot of that stems from being a creature of the earth. George and Milo are not dragons, but they are powerful beings. They get their magic the same as us, from all the elements that make magic for the world."

The two of them spoke for several more minutes before George joined them. He opened her fridge and closed it. When he opened it the second time, he could see that it had been filled. Taking out the stuff to make subs, George told them what he knew.

"First of all, I want to let you know that your fridge is magical. I believe all of ours are, and there isn't any reason for you to do without. Whatever you want will appear in it. Including juice, which, no matter if Milo is your mate or not, you'll need to drink more of. Magic is draining." He set a thick roast beef sub in front of Theo and a meatball one in front of Jamie. "Milo is resting now. No longer in the deep sleep he'd been in. Just having the iron taken from his body is making him feel a great deal better. I've not bothered talking to Winnie. She'll let us know when she knows what happened."

Again, they talked for a while. Pem joined them when they moved to the parlor. After a while, the rest of the family showed up, each of them checking on Milo to see if he was all right. Mom and Dad had been informed and said they would be there soon. He felt terrible that they'd been here so much. Maybe they'd move here soon. That would be great.

Supper was ordered when it became apparent that no one wanted to leave just yet. Jamie, for all her liking quiet time, was doing well with all of them there. He hoped that Milo was her mate. It would be epic to have them together.

~*~

Milo didn't move around too much. It wasn't that he couldn't, but he was achy. He'd never experienced anything like this before. Lily had brought him some clothing from his house, and he had thought about taking a shower. Even the thought of getting out of bed again after going to the bathroom made him want to nap again. Lily asked him if he was all right.

"I'm sure I am. I just feel like I've been run over. I never understood that saying before today. Christ, I do feel like exactly that has been done to me." Lily laid her head on his forehead and told him he was no longer as hot. "Good. That means I'm not feverish anymore."

That had startled him, having a fever. Even as a child, he'd never been sick. Never had anything close to a fever. Nor had he fought a cold. He thought this was the reason he felt so sore. It had never happened to him before.

The lady of the house hadn't been to see him since he'd woken up. His brothers had. So had Rachel and Pem. He'd thought she was avoiding him, but Lily assured him that she was very busy taking a test. It had taken him asking his brothers what sort of test would take so much time, and it turned out she was simply studying for her board exams, not just taking a test.

"She's going to work in the hospital. Run the entire surgery department for us." He asked Theo if Pem was going to work there as well. "I've not asked her directly, but I think that is her plan. The two of them together have been making adjustments to the plans that even the architect is impressed with. Also, you'll be glad to know it'll be easier going green with this project. Solar panels are going to be on most of the roof, as well as one-quarter of the back lot. Having all that land is going to save a great deal of money in the way of heating and cooling."

Milo told Theo about the things he'd been able to unearth where he'd been. Getting in and out of computers had always been something he'd been very good at. Apparently, in the office they ran—it took care of their massive amounts of donations—the computers had been bogged down with not just games, but movies and personal information that was slowing the computers to the point of them not running as well as they all knew they should have been.

"The program I designed will not only keep them from using the computers for anything personal, but now that they have to log in and out of the Internet with their cards, it will make sure they're working when they should be. I was amazed to find out that almost sixty percent of their time was spent on shopping and browsing the Internet. No wonder it takes them so long to get back to us on payroll questions."

Theo had come to see him a couple of times today, earlier that morning and then just a few minutes after he'd gotten his clothing from Lily. Milo was worried he was taking Theo from whatever he had been doing, but his brother assured him that Pem was studying too, and he was bored. He wasn't sure how to take himself being a replacement for boredom, but he didn't comment.

"I wanted to see how you were feeling now. I know I was here only a couple of hours ago, but there are some things I'd like you to help me out with. Just questions mostly, but I could use your input on them." Milo sat up straighter in the bed and felt better for it. "Also, you should know that I've spoken to Jamie. She's been in and out of here while you were sleeping. She's going to come and see you later tonight. But she really is working hard."

"You guys still think she's my mate?" Theo said he didn't think she was. "Why is that? I mean, don't you want me to have a beautiful wife too?"

"Nah, nothing like that. But she's been here with you, in and out, and neither of you seems to be foaming at the mouth to be together." That made him laugh, and he was sure that was what Theo intended for him to do. "Not only that, but she's more like you than I thought. Quiet and reserved. She doesn't even own a television. Not that it's a deal-breaker, but she seems to just not care what is going on in the world around her. I think she's always been that way. I keep getting sidetracked when I go to ask Pem about her."

"I bet you do."

They laughed again when someone knocked at the door. Milo pulled the covers up over his bare chest when he bid the person entry. He'd bet anything that the woman standing there was Jamie.

"Hello."

Chapter 2

Milo moved around the upper level he'd been on and saw that most of the rooms up here were bedrooms, large ones that had a full bath in each of them. He didn't know for sure, but he'd bet that Jamie had had the faeries work on the house, and it was just the way she'd wanted it. Milo had to admit, her tastes ran right alongside of his.

He also discovered a set of back stairs that led up to another floor. Upon inspection of the stairs, going only about halfway up, he knew it more than likely was a staff area. Venturing any further wasn't something he felt comfortable doing, as he didn't know if she had staff in the house or not.

The windows from the back bedrooms, like the one he'd been staying in, had the most beautiful view of the backyard. To say it was simply beautiful would have been grossly understated. The gardens and there were plenty of them, were well maintained and kept up. There was a pool, as well as a pool house. Also, Milo could see the tops of what he thought was a barn, as well as two other homes. Since they seemed to be smaller than the house he was currently in, he assumed they were also servants' homes. Standing at the top of the double staircase, he wondered how far he could make it today without being so exhausted he had to crawl back up the stairs to rest. Today, however, he was determined to make it.

"What the hell do you think you're doing?" He looked down the curved staircase just as he was ready to take the first step. "I thought you were told to rest. I don't think tackling this staircase is resting, do you?"

"I can't stand to be in the house for one more minute." Milo knew he sounded whiney. He was feeling the pressure of not being able to work, be out of doors, or simply able to have a long conversation with someone about nothing. "Please. I need to get out of there before my head explodes. Besides, we've not tried to see if I'm your mate or not. I, for one, would love to find out."

"Me too." She started up the stairs and stopped about halfway up. "I told you yesterday that I don't want to get too close to you in the event you're going to jump my bones. I don't think that would do either of us any good. Well, it might, now that I think about it, but I have to study, and you need to rest. All right?"

"Yes, I understand. I promise not to strip you down to your skin until I have more strength than a newborn. I can't promise I won't kiss you, but that's about all I'm up for at the moment."

She seemed to be thinking on his promise before she came the rest of the way up the stairs. As soon as she was close enough to wrap her arm around his waist, he knew that she was his everything.

Traveling down the stairs slowly seemed to be just what he needed. Once or twice he had to stop, not because he needed to rest, but because of his excitement. Whether or not it was for Jamie or being free, he didn't know, but just the thought of being in the sunshine made his heart beat a little faster.

"You're my mate, aren't you?" He nodded as he stood at the bottom of the stairs. "I thought as much. Yesterday when you were in the bedroom I could smell the earth. Since I'd only just come in from the outdoors, I tried to convince myself that was all it was. Not that I'm pissy about this. I think it'll be all right. But I'm not like other women you might have dated."

"Christ, I hope not." He'd meant it as a joke, but she glared at him. "I'm sorry. That didn't come out right. The kind of women I usually date are women that know my family has a great deal of money, and that's what they're hoping for. Me to marry them and set them up for life. However, of late, I haven't been doing much of anything but working."

"Me too. I take my state boards tomorrow for Texas." They were moving through the living room, and he paused a moment to look around the room. "I don't know what your tastes are, but if you want to change anything, this room is off-limits. I mean, it's a room I've always wanted, and if you don't mind, I'll put you another room in if I have to so I can have this one to myself."

"I love it. The furniture looks soft and cozy. I'm in love with the fireplace too. The mantle just screams for some family photos on it." He moved past Jamie to look at the painting over the mantle. "This is this house, isn't it?"

"Yes. I don't know where the faeries found it, but I love it hanging there. They must have cleaned it up as well. It looks freshly painted. You can see that the house has been added onto a few times. Like the wings at the back of the house there. The pool, too, of course. But the picture has a year on the back that I found. It was painted in the late seventeen hundreds." He touched his fingers to the paint and jerked his hand away. "I was going to warn you about that. Somewhere along the line, I discovered I can touch things too and get a great deal from it. I try hard not to do that—it's kind of freaky."

He put his hand back to the painting and closed

his eyes as the house as it was now began to change, going backward to be the painting he was touching. When he moved his hand forward, just a little at a time, he was able to tell Jamie what he was seeing.

"The woman who painted this picture was named Nelly James Darkhouse. Did you know she was part Native American?" Jamie sat down on one of the couches and told him she knew that. It was in the big family Bible in the library. "Well, smarty pants, did you know that she and her tribe were somewhat magical. The Darkhouses, I mean."

"Now that, I didn't know. When her brother, who lived in the house, died sometime after his wife, Nelly, moved into the house with her husband. She had eleven children, but sadly only four lived past their fourth birthday. I'm named for her." Milo nodded as he sat down beside her on the couch. "When the house was finished, she gave birth to a son, James Darkhouse. He was the first of many children born and raised here until her death years later. Also, many years later, her husband, for some unknown reason, killed himself by hanging himself from the rafters in the barn."

"The one in the back of this property?" She told him it had been long since torn down in the name of expansion. "I guess that's both good and sad. What else do you know, and I can fill in the blanks?"

"Nothing much. My parents were only children

of only children. But for as far back as anyone can remember, there were lots of children born to each family except mine. When they had my sister, I was already old enough to be out of the house. Not really old enough, but I did go away to college when I was just sixteen." He said he had been that way as well. "I know a lot about you from your family. You're so much like me I didn't think we'd be a pair. You know the old saying, opposites attract?"

"Yes, well, perhaps this is better for the two of us." She looked up at the picture, and he did as well. "You said there was only one child born per family. Do you know if they were all men then? I mean, no one changed the name of this place to theirs in all this time."

"They weren't all sons, but every time a daughter was born, the father of the bride would insist that the male change his name to Darkhouse. I have no idea why that worked for them. I have no intentions of making anyone change their name for the sake of a big house." She laughed. "Unless you want to, that is."

"Not particularly. But that doesn't mean we have to change the house name, does it?" She shook her head. "What else can you tell me about this home?"

"I never liked living here. I do now, but when I was a child, I hated this place. It was dark and cold. Mostly to do with my parents. They didn't particularly care for sharing their life with someone like me." He asked her what she meant. "I was a wild child. I will admit I was in trouble more than my share. But when I signed up for the service, I think they were thrilled to be rid of me. I know I was in getting away from here."

They talked about their lives. Mostly it was her family that was talked about, as his family had filled her in on him for the most part. When she asked him if he was ready to go outdoors, he agreed. But she didn't need to help him now. Just sitting with her had given him the extra strength he needed.

There was a large box on the deck where they were. It looked like she was putting together a grill. What made him laugh was that she was using a different language than English to read the instructions. Watching her while she did exactly what she'd read, he looked around the backyard from this level.

He could see that someone had recently mowed. As he watched, he saw a herd of snowy white goats come out from under the trees. As they headed to the deck, Jamie stood up and pointed to the back of the yard again. Milo could tell they were dejected at not being allowed to come any closer to the house, and he asked her about it.

"I won't get anything done if they come up here again. They'll eat the instructions too. That's why I'm using the French instructions, as they ate the English ones. Not to mention, I had to follow them around for an hour until one of them shit out the missing screw they'd eaten." Milo couldn't help it. He was laughing so hard he felt his ribs ache from it. "You'd not think it was so funny if you were sitting here like I am, and all of a sudden, one of them was right on top of your back like some kind of fucking king of the hill."

Begging her to stop, he could see that she was smiling at him. "I needed that, Jamie. My mom says that laughter is the best kind of medicine." Jamie sat up when she had all but the lid put on the grill. "I take it you like to grill out, and that's why this thing is so big."

"I do, actually. But when I saw the way your family eats, I decided I could cook for us should you want and be able to put extras in the fridge for later." She looked up at him. "Your brother George is going to get his face knocked in by some woman one day, but he made it so that my fridge is full all the time. I sometimes like to just cook things for myself."

"I love anything and everything that comes from cooking outdoors." She said she was going to cook them salmon tonight. "Do you cook much?"

"Not so much. I'm better at eating those things that come prepackaged like you get in the service. That way, it's easy to clean up too. Though, just feeding me, it's not been so bad." When the lid was put on, she moved the grill to the other side of the deck before having a seat. "I forgot to tell you that your parents are coming the day after tomorrow. They were going to come yesterday, but Finn asked them to wait a couple of days. Just until Pem and I are finished up with our tests. She'll ace it, but I have to study a little harder. Not too much, but I think I'll do all right."

"I have a feeling you're going to ace it as well." She grinned at him. "How far along is the hospital now? I'm betting it's close to being finished."

"It is. I guess the builders are aware that they're only doing the outside, and the rest is done by the faeries. To hurry things along. There is a huge need for a hospital around here. I think it's at least fifty miles to the closest one, and it's not anything but an emergency room from what I've heard." He nodded, knowing that was exactly what it was. "Where do we go from here, you and I?"

"Forward. I'm hoping. I have to admit to you, I'm enjoying getting to know you. To hear your family history. You said my family told you all about ours." She told him they'd told her more about him than their history. "I guess they'd do that. I heard a great deal about you too, from Pem. She and you sound like you were hellions in the service. I also heard about your sister."

"Missy. She was born with a handicap that is hereditary. Finn explained to me that I'd not have the gene to pass along to my children, should you want to have any." He said it was up to her. It was her body. "Don't fucking do that, all right? Just don't. Don't try and make me have to make decisions all the time. You're a grown assed man, and you have to have opinions too, or this shit is going to get old. If I ask you something, I want you to fucking answer me. Not fob all over things by saying 'it's your body.' Do you want children or not? It's simple enough, don't you think?"

"Yes, I'd like to have children with you." Milo laughed. "Are you always this testy about things, or is this an off day?"

"Off day, I guess. I'm sorry. I know what it is you're saying to me, and thank you for that, but I do want your input on things like money. I know you have a great deal of it—so do I. Are you the type of person that gets all macho and has to make sure all the bills are paid or are you the kind of guy that says I'll pay for half, you the other half? Neither one is anything I'm going to like." Milo loved seeing her all worked up. "You might want to have an opinion about right now."

"My money is your money, and I'm assuming it's the same with yours." She nodded and leaned back on the chair she was on. The goats started inching their way toward them now that she had finished the grill. "My aunt Carson said she took care of a lot of things for you while I was down. If anyone can make things work, it would be her. She's well connected."

"I am as well, believe it or not. So is Pem, but not like I am. My dad was good friends with a previous president. I think you know the one I'm talking about. He was a schmuck like my father. I suppose it could be considered a good or bad thing that he died in office. But when I got out of the service due to being so ill, the current president called me to ask if there was anything he could do for me. A few days ago, he called again to tell me that he was happy I'd hooked up with the Mannings. I guess you're a big deal." Milo didn't say anything. He didn't think he was, but his family was. "Anyway, I have to take this test tomorrow, and then I'm going to see about getting things worked out with the houses in the back. Your mom—she doesn't know, by the way, that we're mates as yet—but she said I'd be better off hiring a staff. I suppose she's right, but I don't dirty too much up around here."

"No, I wouldn't see you leaving a mess behind. But I can see where my mom is right. Having a staff with my family will make it, so you're not cooking all the time for them. Or ordering out. Whatever you've been doing when they're over." She told him they were on their own when they all arrived at once. Milo laughed. "They've only been in all at one time when you were first brought here. By the way, the room you're sleeping in right now is not the master. I've not been sleeping in it either, so you know. It's a big fucking room."

"Would you share the room with me tonight?"

She looked at the goats before answering him. When she nodded, Milo felt like he'd run a marathon. Jamie watched the goats a little more before standing up.

"I'm not sure I'm ready for sex just yet. I have a lot going on, and some of it has to do with the fact that I'm no longer going to die. All right?" He nodded. "All right. I'm going to fix us some dinner. I mean, start on it. Anyway, I don't know if I have nearly enough for your entire family, not without overworking the magic on the fridge. But if you'd like to let them know we're mates, I guess we can order out again." He nodded. "I'm assuming that once they hear that, they'll be on us like white on rice?"

"Yes, I'm betting you're right on that."

She went into the house, and Milo saw that one of the goats had gotten in behind Jamie. When it came running out of the house with her hot on his hooves, he had to laugh again while reaching for his mom.

I'm assuming you feel better? He told her he did, as a matter of fact. *And Jamie, she's not thrown you out yet?*

Doubtful that she will, she's my mate. He thought he would hear his mom's screams of happiness for the rest of his life. *Would you like to come here today and bring food for us to have for dinner tonight? We don't have a staff yet, but we've been talking.*

I'll see what I can do. In the meantime, I'll see what I can do about getting everyone there. He thanked her. *Oh, Milo, I'm so happy for you two. She's a wonderful person. A little outspoken even for me, but I love her.*

I think I do as well, Mom.

He closed the connection when she said she'd be by later. He went into the house to tell Jamie they'd be having company. It didn't even occur to him that he'd yet to touch her until he saw her in the kitchen rinsing off the salmon. He was going to take care of that as soon as he could.

~*~

Jamie made her way out to the deck. Just as she closed the door behind her, the goats came up on the deck to be with her. The stupid things were adorable and annoying, but she wasn't regretting having them on the land. The faeries loved them as well. Jangles was riding one of them when he came to the porch where she was sitting. He made himself comfortable on the other chair across from her.

"My lady, I do believe they've fertilized the land here better than the truck that came to that man's house across from you. And they trim up the grass nicely as well, don't you think?" She explained to Jangles it was a service. "Yes, Lord Milo explained it to me this morn. I thought the Mannings were coming over tonight to celebrate. Have they changed their mind, perhaps?"

"They're here now. I'm just taking a break from them. They're very loud and touchy." Jangles told her that was the dragon in them. "Whatever it is, I've been alone for most of my life, and I need a break from them once — What the hell is that thing that's riding one of my goats? And what has he done to her?"

Milo joined her when Jangles was laughing so hard he couldn't answer her. The little man was literally rolling on the ground, he was losing it so badly. She might have enjoyed his mirth but for the fact that the creature, whatever it was, had turned her goat to — well, a rainbow-colored little guy. When Milo joined him, laughing at the sight himself, she made her way out to the yard to confront whatever the thing was that was hanging onto the goat's horns and riding him like a bronco.

"What are you doing?" She sat down when the little creature looked at her. She still had no idea what it was, but it was beginning to look more and more human-like as she sat there. "Did you hurt my goat?"

"Nay, my lady. I was only having a bit of fun with her. You are the new mistress to the Manning Dragons, are you not?" She didn't answer him. Frankly, since she didn't know him, she wasn't sure she should even be this close to him. "I am a pixie.

We're bigger than the faeries and fae around here. I am Lord Color."

"You're not a lord of anything, Color. I've explained that to you before." Milo sat on the ground next to her. "While I'm sure the goat had fun with you riding her, you shouldn't be changing her colors to suit yourself. It startled my mate."

"I can see that. But if she doesn't believe she's having fun, she should ask her. I've been asking before I play my tricks, Lord Milo. I promised you I would, and I have. Go ahead, ask Millie if she was having a bit of fun with me." She asked him who Millie was. "Why, the goat, Mistress. They all have names. You only have to ask, and they'll tell you. Like they did me."

"I'm just supposed to say, 'Hey Millie, are you having fun being different colors?' Like that is going to—"

"Oh Mistress, it is so fun to have Color on my back. He gives me such fun. And the colors are like the rainbow in the sky." Jamie looked at Milo and back at Millie. "You can understand all manner of creatures. Did no one tell you that?"

"No, I don't think anyone knows I could—" She looked at Milo. "Are you doing this? Making me insane by my thinking I'm speaking to a...to Millie?"

"You can understand her?" She nodded, and Millie climbed up into her lap. It was both comforting and scary to have the little goat in her arms. "I can't do that. I'm not even sure any of us can do that. We can talk to the faeries, the brownies too, but not the four-legged creatures that are around. Let me see if it works on other animals."

"I'd rather you didn't tell your family. I don't want them to think I'm any stranger than I am." She heard the door open and looked up to see that they were all on the deck. "You already did."

"I asked if anyone could speak to animals. I'm sorry. But they're happy. This can be extremely helpful to us in a lot of areas." The only way she could think of it helping was putting her away in an institution someplace near her sister. "Mom wants you to see if you can call to a bird. Any of them."

"Sure. And when the bird doesn't land in front of me, you're going to have me locked up." He told her he loved her. Jamie looked at him for several seconds. "Do you really love me, Milo?"

"With all that I am." When he kissed her on the mouth, Jamie felt like she could conquer the world. "I don't know what you'd have to do, but see if you can call something to you. Whatever you wish."

Standing up after letting Millie go, she went to the trees at the back of the property. There was a nesting group of falcons there that had been coming back since she could remember to have their babies. Looking to where she thought they might be, she called to the bird and asked one of them to come to her.

The beautiful bird landed in front of her. She sat down hard and startled him enough that he bounced back just a little. When he asked her if she was all right, all Jamie could do was nod at him.

"You are the mistress of Lord Milo." She told him she was and that her name was Jamie Manning. "I am Hawk. My mate, her name is Lady. We have been ever so grateful to you for allowing our kind to breed here. It is as safe a place as we have ever been. Thank you, my lady."

"I can understand you." He bowed again at her and then hopped closer. "I don't know what to do right now. I'm a little freaked out. I was told the Mannings use that word a great deal."

"Can you understand him?" She nodded at Milo when he sat down beside her. "Good. Would you mind asking him a few things for me? I would love to know how we can help his kind and others have plenty of food and shelter, so we don't lose out on their kind."

She asked Hawk. "He said that what you are doing now, with leaving the trees where they stand and leaving the fallen where they lay, helps them a great deal. Hawk said the only thing he'd wish for is that there was more drinkable water." She looked beyond where they were sitting. "There used to be a pond in the back of this property. I don't know what sort of shape it's in, but I can have it cleaned up for you. No chemicals, however."

"That would be wonderful, my lady. Also, if I remember, there used to be a lovely fountain on the land. I believe it was just where we are sitting. If that could be returned, that would be helpful as well. You've no idea how much we enjoyed that when we were younger. All manner of animals in this forest have missed it."

She told Milo, and he said he'd put the faeries right on it.

"I have a picture of it in the house. It wasn't here when I was living at home, so I didn't think about it when I saw the photo a few days ago." Milo asked her if she wanted it to look the same. "I think I do. It was, if I remember, a beautiful fountain with three or four tiers that had flowers all around the lowest bowl. I remember thinking it had some very detailed flowers around it. I believe I'd like to have some fish in it, too. That way, if one of the animals needs something to eat, they could take them. Or not. It would be there if necessary."

"Thank you, Mistress. If it is all right with you and your mate, I should like to come to speak with you more often. It is a pleasure to know there are dragons about and that someone can help us when we need it. I will serve you in any way you wish. You need only to allow me to nip your skin gently, and I'll be able to speak to you as we are now when we are not together. You can call for me at any time then."

Without any hesitation, she put her hand out to him. When he flapped his wings, she was distracted enough for him to have bitten her and back away. While it was painful, it only lasted for a moment. Bidding her good night, he left them there to return to his mate.

Jamie looked at Milo. "I'm officially freaked the fuck out."

With that, she fainted dead away. The day had just been too much for her. The strong arms around her penetrated her overworked mind, and Jamie knew for the first time in a very long time that she was safe. Not just from the world, but everything that had ever been a part of her life.

Chapter 3

Winnie tested the iron she'd removed from Milo's body to see if it would tell her anything about it. Nothing had been found other than a few pieces of it in his hotel room when Milo had been away. Even the place he'd been working had nothing in it that would tell her one of the employees there had given it to him. Just as she was putting it away to think about something else, Jamie joined her in the office she'd been using.

"I have to ask you something. Not that I think I can do what you do, but this tastes funny to me. Can you tell me if you think it's off, or am I reading too much into this shit?" When Jamie handed her the cup of tea, Winnie could smell the iron in it even before she sipped it. Looking at the younger woman, she asked her where she'd gotten it. "Milo. He said he'd gotten it as a gift last year from one of the people he worked with on some computer stuff. It's poison, isn't it?"

"Yes. But not in the sense that it will poison him now. Did he tell you who gave it to him?" Jamie handed her a Christmas card and sat down across from her at the large desk. "You're not going to be affected by that any longer. Neither will George or Milo. I took care of that little mishap for them, so you can drink it if you wish."

"No thanks. I'm not a huge fan of tea anyway. I don't mind it, but I don't really care for it. Do you know who that person is? Milo doesn't remember them, but he's looking through his notes now." Winnie put the card and the iron away and regarded the woman across from her. "Do I have shit on my face or something? You're staring at me as if I might have. What is it? Just so you know, I'm slightly afraid of you but not nearly as much as I am, Cindi. Talking to the dead? No the fuck way. What is it you're sizing me up for? A coffin?"

"No. What thoughts you have in your head at times. No, I was thinking about how you were able to track this down for me. I'd still be looking if not for your help." She said she only asked her about the tea. "Yes. But I wouldn't have thought of it as a gift from someone. And to answer your question, it is from the same man that is running the IT department at the place Milo had been working just recently."

"Do you think he meant to kill him?" Winnie explained to her what she'd gotten when she was handed the card. "So he drinks this to put more iron in his own blood. I don't know if it works that way, but there have been stranger things people have done in the name of health. So now what do you do? I would guess you'd have to tell Milo that he can't drink any more gifts from people. If you don't, I will. In the event you didn't notice, I don't have a lot of trust in people. They're all out to get something, it seems."

"Do you think we are? The Mannings, I mean?" Instead of answering her right away, Jamie got up and poured the tea out the open doors onto the grass. When she sat back down, she had a very unreadable look on her face. "Tell me what you're thinking. Just so you know, unless you cause harm to one of the dragons, I can't harm you. And that would include hurting Milo."

"First of all, I wouldn't hurt him for my life. Secondly, I don't think I trust anyone any more than you do. But in answer to your question, the answer is twofold. Are the Mannings out for something? Yes. Yes, you are. To give back to the community as much as you can. In order to do that, you take liberties with their minds and hack into computers to make it happen. Cheating, I think that would be called. Do I trust them? You? Yes. I don't know why, but I do. Milo and Pem as well. The others, I really don't know.

I know what I've been told about them, all of them. But as far as trust, I don't have a great deal of it for many people."

"What if I told you they'd lay down their lives for you?" Jamie asked her why they'd do that. "Because we protect one another with our lives. Even though we're all immortal, we'd still go to great lengths to make sure you were as safe as we can make you."

"I don't have any kind of thoughts on that, to be honest with you." Jamie looked around the room, then back at her. "My parents lived in this house from the day they were married until they were killed. And before them, my grandparents all the way back as far as anyone can count. I hated it here. Hated not just the walls that seemed to be crushing me all the time, but everything about this place. It was just a house to me. Then I met you guys."

"Now you have a home." Jamie nodded. "I don't understand what that has to do with what I asked you."

"Only one person has ever made me feel like I was worth laying their lives down for. Not my parents. It was my grandmother when she was living with us. I'm still looking for where they put her. Some cheap nursing home, I'm betting. Not even my sister supported me, though it's no fault of her own." Winnie was beginning to understand Jamie a bit more. More than Milo did, she'd bet. "I don't trust because I really didn't know how until I met Pem. Did she tell you we nearly died one day while working? That's why she was given an honorable discharge. Then after that, the nightmares were too much, and they made her depression worse."

"What happened?" Winnie wasn't sure she was going to answer her but didn't want to have to pry either. Whatever it was, she thought both of them were still having nightmares about it. "I think it might help you to tell me."

"That's what the shrink told me. But to tell it, I don't know...it makes it seem all the more like it really fucking did happen." Jamie got up and picked up the framed ribbon she was sure had been on her uniform at one time. "We were just taking a break after nineteen hours of working. It was grueling and exhausting, but since we were the only two that qualified for working on the front line, we were working our asses off." Winnie wondered why they weren't on the ship they'd been assigned to. "Some fuckweed decided we'd be better off working close at hand with the wounded. So instead of leaving us where we needed to be all along, Pem and I and ten others were shipped to the front. Pem and I were the only two that made it back."

Winnie didn't search her mind, but she did look through her own to find the incident that would have been the one Jamie was talking about. When she thought she'd found it, Jamie started talking again.

"We were in the mess tent having a cup of what was supposed to have been hot cocoa. It was nothing more than hot brown water, but it was all there was as the cook had been killed three days before. The people in the tent with us weren't speaking either — it was just quiet, you know. Like the fucked up shit that happens before the shit hits the fan." Winnie knew Jamie had never told anyone this before. It wasn't in any of her records with the doctor she'd been seeing before or the one she was seeing here. Neither had Pem, it appeared. "The machine that was making coffee exploded first. That wasn't anything new for the shit that we had. Nothing worked all that well, so when it started spraying the liquid all over the ground, none of us even moved. Then the man at the table across from us, his head just disappeared. I think it took me a few seconds of disbelief before I grabbed Pem. We ducked under the table and watched as three more people hit the ground. There was a lot of screaming. The sound was much worse once it was cut off, like when the person was killed. The shots being fired weren't coming from inside the tent, but from the outdoors where the other soldiers and doctors were, we came to realize." Jamie paused, then started again. "It seemed like forever that we were ducked under the table. Pem and I held onto each other, knowing the very next shot was going to take us both out."

Winnie could see it happening in Jamie's mind. Tapping into the memory gave her an insight that was much more horrific than the way Jamie was telling it. There was no pause in the shooting. And if asked, she'd bet Jamie would have been able to tell someone what sort of weapons had been used throughout the shootings. There had been four, and someone tossing grenades as well. When Jamie started talking again, she knew this was the part where her trust in people had been lost.

"Mail had arrived just before the end of our shift. Nothing for either of us, of course. No one cared where we were and what we were doing. Doubtful if anyone even would have cared if we'd been killed that day. Anyway, mail had brought a lot of news for the men in charge. Two of them, I guess, had been given *Dear John* letters. It was what set off the captain and the two lieutenants that were in charge of the unit. I don't know who the fourth man was, but they had decided they'd had enough of being in a war that had taken their families away. Their words, not mine." Winnie quietly asked her what had happened. "They came into the mess tent to celebrate. I suppose we could have stayed hidden, and they might well have never known we were there. But I had to know. I had to know why they'd done something so horrific."

Winnie watched as it unfolded in her mind. Saw the exact moment that Jamie had decided she was going to make sure these men paid for what they'd done. Standing up, she confronted the men and asked them what the bloody fuck they were doing.

"Lookee, Ben, we missed one." The lieutenant aimed his weapon at Jamie when she asked them what they were doing a second time. "We're ending the war for a lot of people, Jamie. They'll all get to go home and be with their families."

"You killed these people so they could go home? What fucked up kind of logic is that? They're fucking dead, you morons. You killed them for no reason." The man pointing his gun at her told her that he was going home too. "Good for you, fucktard. In a bag or upright? Either way, you've murdered a lot of soldiers. For what? What sort of reason could you have for killing innocent men and women?"

Jamie had moved away from Pem, leaving her on the ground. Pem stayed where she was while Jamie spoke to the four men.

"We told you so that they can go home to their families." The man, Lieutenant Parlor, laughed with his buddies as he stood up and moved toward her. The gun was at her head as he continued. "You're a nice fine piece of ass, now aren't you, Doc? Why don't you show us what you have underneath that uniform? Maybe I'll give you a quicky death."

The movement was quick, and Winnie was impressed. Not only did she kill Parlor, but she also managed to kill two of the other three by snapping Parlor's neck and using his weapon to shoot the others. Once they were dead, still holding Parlor in front of her, Jamie was shot twice before Pem shot and killed the fourth man with a weapon she'd picked up from one of the dead on the ground.

When Jamie had told Winnie that she and Pem were the only two that survived, she wasn't kidding. Of the fifty-three men and women at the unit that day, they were the only two that had been able to walk away.

"Pem operated on me while I was lying there with my gun, watching over us. The entire time she was doing it, she was berating me for taking such a chance. It took three days before anyone came to check on us and another two before anyone decided to not blame us for the number of deaths. It might have been a shorter time, but the major in charge hadn't called anyone in when he realized there was trouble going on, He had thought, like most people with a dick and no brains would, that he'd be able to rectify what the hell was going on." Winnie didn't say anything as the younger woman came back to sit down. "These men were fighting for us, or they were supposed to be. Not only did they kill all the men and women there with us, but they thought it was one big fucking joke. I don't trust anyone but a handful of people to have my back. I'm sorry if that isn't what you want to hear, but that's the way it rocks for me."

"I understand. However, I do hope you'll give us a chance to be there for you should it ever come to that. Not only am I better at keeping you safe, but I'm also more experienced at it." Jamie told her she wasn't stupid. "No, I'd say you're very intelligent. I wonder if Milo knows just how smart you really are. Does anyone, including Pem, know that?"

"It's never come up." Nodding, Winnie decided she'd not tell anyone of this conversation unless asked by Cooper. He was the only person she had to tell if he questioned her. "Are we good here? I have some shit to do today, and I was wondering if you're going to be around."

"Here? No, I wasn't. Is it necessary that I am?" Jamie said she didn't care one way or the other, but since Milo was gone as well, she didn't want her thinking they'd abandoned her. "I don't think that. But I do appreciate you telling me. Anything I can help you with?"

"I don't know. What do you know about corporate buyouts?" Winnie decided even if she didn't know shit about whatever Jamie was doing today, she'd still go with her. "I have to go to one of the businesses I own and figure out why the head of the company thinks I should sell out."

"I'd love to go."

They were headed out the door when Winnie

heard from Carson. She didn't pause to listen to the woman but got into the car with Jamie. They were on the road when Carson finally got to the point.

I need you to go by the new hospital. Something is going on with one of the walls that is giving the architect some issues. I can't even begin to wonder what the hell he's talking about, but there is something going on with the electrical. Can you check it out? She told her she had Jamie with her. *She might be able to make heads or tails out of it better than I am over the phone. I don't want to have to go there and kick this guy's ass to make him understand he's not good at explaining shit to people.*

They headed there first. Jamie told her she could get her shit done later, but the electrical, whatever it was, sounded more important than buyouts. Winnie hoped it was a simple fix for them both, but she had Carson check on the issue Jamie was having. While she did that, she and Jamie went to the sixth floor to see what could be going on.

~*~

Jamie tried listening to the manager telling her what he was thinking when he'd set up a meeting with a couple of different buyers for himself. It was only one of the many businesses her family had owned prior to their deaths.

"You see, when your parents were alive, they just let me do what I wanted when it came to the business. It has worked out well for us since the beginning of my tenure here." He smiled, but it wasn't all that reassuring. Winnie didn't say anything, but Jamie could tell she was one second from killing the man. "You must not bother yourself with this, Jamie. As I said, I have everything under control here. However, if you'd give me the name of the person who called you in on this, I will make sure they know not to bother you again."

"I want to be bothered." He shook his head at her. "This is my company, correct? I'm the one that pays your check, as well as funds this place when it needs it. Is that correct?"

"It is correct, but as I have said to you many times now, it's not necessary for you to bother with this. I have it well under control." She asked him again who was the buyer and what they were paying. "You see, that's you bothering with this again. I have all the specs in my office. It's going to go smoothly, and once the buyout is taken care of, we won't have to use your money any longer."

"I'm not going to ask you again, Mr. Huber. Who the fuck is thinking they're going to buy my company from me?" He told her, finally, that it was a warehousing firm by the name of Nelson Wholesale. "Why is a wholesale business wanting to purchase a company that makes boxes for jewelry and small, expensive items? That is what we do here, correct? I have the specs, as you called them, right here. And nowhere on it does it mention any other things we sell that are on this list that Nelson sells. What is it they think they're going to do with this company that will help them?"

"Well, when are you leaving so I can handle this?" Huber looked at Winnie when she cleared her throat. Jamie was still waiting on the man to continue when Winnie had done that. Jamie thought for sure she was going to tell her if she let it go, she was going to rip her a new ass. Sort of. But she wasn't going to be happy.

Make him tell you. Jamie frowned, and Winnie winked. *Demand that he tells you what you want to know. I think you have an idea as to what it is. Just make him answer you. All you need to do that is in your head now. Just do it.*

She looked at Huber again and could see that he was sweating. Profusely. When he mopped his handkerchief across his forehead, he said he was going to go and let her and her friend work it out.

He has no idea who I'm mated to. Nor does he know you. Winnie told her that in this, it didn't matter. But she could make him tell her everything, including the type of sex he loved. *No thanks. All right. But you'll bail me out if I fuck this up.*

You won't, Jamie. You're going to be just fine. She hoped so. Jamie had seen firsthand what raping someone's mind could do to them. *Go for it.*

"You know what? I've had enough of your shit. Tell me right now what the fuck is going on with my company, and I want the truth. All of it." She could see the man struggling with not answering her. Jamie didn't even feel bad when blood started to stream down his chin from biting his lips. "Tell me."

She could feel it then, the compulsion she'd put into the last part of her demand. When he started sobbing, saying what was going on, she was too shocked to understand him until he started to repeat himself.

"She made me do it. Momma said the only way I was going to amount to anything was to sell this stupid company to her brother, then she'd allow me back into her good graces. My momma can be so mean when it strikes her, and I just couldn't say no any longer. It's not like anyone ever showed up here before now. Who would have known what I was doing until it was too late? No one, that's who. Now here you are making demands, and my mom is going to be so pissed off at me that she'll lock me out of the house again." Jamie asked him how old he was. "Fifty-seven. What does that have to do with anything? What Momma wants, Momma gets. She's so mean to me. I need this to work, Ms. Darkhouse. It has got to. I don't want to be left out of my mom's house anymore. Just go home, and I'll have it all finished up in no time. Please? I beg of you. Let me make my momma happy."

Winnie looked as surprised as she did when Jamie glanced over at her. He was selling her company to his uncle so that his momma would be happy? At fucking fifty-seven years of age? What the mother fucking hell?

"This right here is why I have trust issues." Winnie laughed, and Jamie turned back to Huber. "You're fired. As of this very moment, you will have your desk cleaned out and your possessions sent to you—and only what belongs to you. I would like your badge right now."

He was sobbing as he turned it over to her, telling her again how unhappy his mother was going to be. Winnie called security for her, and after telling them what she wanted, Huber was escorted out of the building while she sat there thinking about what the hell had just happened.

Do you need my help? She looked around for Milo and remembered that he could speak to her. *I can come there after I leave here if you wish. To see what we can do to fix this for you. I'm sorry this happened.*

I am too, but I don't think, now that the sale has been taken care of, that there is anything I have to be on top of. Winnie is here with me. He said that was who had contacted him. *I guess I will have to find someone to come in and run the day to day, but I have a feeling I'm going to have to take more interest in what I'm in charge of.*

That I can help you with. If you get with your attorney and ask them to make you a list of the places you own, the managers' names and things like that, he should be able to do that. I'll have Aunt Carson go over the list to see if any of them are a momma's boy who you might have to fire. Winnie said she'd not had any idea the man was going to say that. She laughed, telling him she'd not either. *I love my mom to pieces, but she'd kick my ass if I was still living at home by fifty-seven and trying to make her happy by espionage.*

I wonder if my parents ever went to the board meetings and such. Right now, I'm thinking not. I was just thinking I'd make a plan to meet with each of them as soon as possible to show them I am not my parents. That should stir up some mommas. They were both laughing when she pulled her notes to her. *I have one more meeting today, then I'm finished. After that, I'm thinking I'd like to have you jump my bones. Or I'm not opposed to jumping yours. It's been a while, so I might need some help.* He was quiet, but she knew he was still listening to her. *Or not. It's not that big of a deal, you know.*

It is to me. Christ, you have no idea how many times I've wanted to hunt you down in that big house and do just that. She asked him what had stopped him. *I didn't want to rush you into anything. Ever.*

And here I thought it was my body odor or something. He told her that he could smell her, and she smelled of home to him. *I'm sorry. I never quite know when it's a good time to make a joke or not. Not that it matters — I still fail at making them. I'd love to share my bed with you. I don't know what's in there right now — in the master bedroom, I mean — but I'm willing to bet if I talk to Jangles, he can make sure we have more than we might need.*

I'm sure he can. Have him work on that for you, and I'll take you out to dinner when I'm finished here. Then I can take you in the limo on the way to the restaurant, in the place, and on the way home, so I'll be ready and not too needy by the time we get home.

When Winnie joined her again, Jamie had already sent Jangles to have someone take care of the master bedroom. She was talking to her attorney, someone else she'd not met yet when Winnie sat across from her. Explaining what she wanted from him seemed to be getting her nowhere until she decided she had enough of getting the runaround.

"I'll be at your office in twenty minutes." Winnie said she could have her there in two seconds. "Better yet, I'm in the lobby now. I want you to be ready with the information I've asked for, or I'm not above firing someone else today. Do you understand me?"

"I don't have time for this." She told Mr. Yankee he'd better be making time. "Well, aren't you just the bossy thing? I'll try and be ready, and if I'm not, you're going to have to wait like everyone else I work with. I don't have time for your drama today." Then the phone went dead.

"He hung up on me." Winnie took the phone from her and put it back in the cradle. "I was going to have you pop me into the lobby, but I think I'd rather just be right up there in his office. Can you do that?"

"I can. It would be my pleasure." Winnie was laughing as she stood up. "I think I'm going to like working with you, Jamie. You certainly like to get to the heart of shit. Here we go."

Jamie didn't know what she had expected when popping into the office, but it certainly wasn't her attorney fucking a woman from the backend and yelling how he was coming. She waited with Winnie until he staggered back before she spoke. It took her two tries to talk over the laughter of Winnie when she finally got her point across.

"Put that little thing away. No one on an empty or full stomach wants to see that thing this early in the morning." He just stared at her as if he'd never seen a woman before. "Oh, do put it away. It's nasty looking and tiny. I want to talk to you about how I'm going to fire you as my attorney. In the event you have your fucking head on straight now, my name is Jamie Darkhouse Manning. Get my files gathered up — by someone else if you please — and I'll let you get back to —" She looked at the woman. "I'm assuming you're not his wife."

"No. His new secretary. I was gonna quit after today anyway. He does have a little cock."

The woman left, telling her that she'd be back with her files. Mr. Yankee continued to sit there with his pants open and his eyes closed. Shaking her head, she left him there when Winnie left.

It was a few seconds later that she heard screams from the office she'd left. Winnie joined her in the front office and told her that Mrs. Yankee was in there now. All hell, she supposed, had just broken loose. But Jamie had her files, so it didn't bother her when Mrs. Yankee left the office with her phone pressed to her ear, calling her attorney, Jamie assumed.

"This is a really fucked up day, don't you think?' Winnie laughed and said she'd had a good time. "Me too, if you want the truth. But now I have to find someone to work for me that won't be bending his help over his desk while on the clock. Know of anyone?"

"I do. But I think you should let one of us take care of it. You've had enough fun for one day." She said she really had. "I'll take you to lunch. The other women, Milo's mother and aunts, are going to meet us. They've already popped into this part of the country to eat with us."

"I don't even care where it's at so long as I can have a large piece of dark chocolate when I'm finished."

They popped into a lovely little bistro and sat down. They must have been expecting them because there were two seats ready for them.

Winnie told them what they'd been up to while Jamie ordered her brownie, a house specialty. After that, she didn't give a shit what else happened to her today. Life was suddenly just peachy. Until tomorrow, she thought. Tomorrow she'd have to make things work out better for herself and Milo. But for now, she was content to have lunch with these women.

Chapter 4

Milo had heard from his mom three times since leaving the office. He'd not made it home, but he was told that the house was ready for him and Jamie. Lily had made sure things were just so for him. Mom had told him how much better a mood Jamie was in after having a dark chocolate brownie.

She seemed to just melt in the seat after having one. I swear to you, it was like watching someone have sex. She enjoyed it so much. He begged his mom not to talk about sex. *Why not? I don't know if you realize this or not, but someone somewhere had to have sex in order for you to be here.*

That's not the point. You're my mother, and there is a breaking point that—just don't talk about sex with me. All right? She laughed, and he had to smile. *I've set up some things to be brought here when you get home. Dad said he thought I'd like to have a few pieces of art that I did when I was in that phase of my life. Also, there are some of his things that he's sending along. Have you spoken to him?*

I have. He's sending some of the things I had saved back from when you were smaller. Not a great deal of things, but some I thought you and Jamie would enjoy seeing. Also, I've been talking to some of the other dragons, and it seems that you and Jamie can have children, but at this point, it's anyone's guess as to what sort of magic they could have. He asked her if they thought he could have a dragon. *No, I'm sorry. Not with her being a human before all her magic. Did you tell me she has no one but her sister in her life? I have been doing some research on a couple of things for her. I think there is more than just the money she inherited from her family estate. It looks like there was a policy from her great-grandmother that hasn't been cashed. I have Carson looking into it. It's a hefty amount of money because of interest being accumulated.*

I know she's going to say she doesn't need it, but I'll let her know as soon as I see her. Not as soon as he saw her, but he would make it a point to tell her at some time. Milo had plans for tonight. Then he remembered why he'd wanted to talk to his mom. *I know you're more than likely looking into this for her, as she said she was going to ask. But do you remember that young boy you scared straight about ten or so years ago? I think his name was Matthew or something.*

Marshall. Marshall Fender. Yes, I remember him well. He is an attorney — oh Milo, what a wonderful idea. Yes, I'll contact him right away. He smiled when his mom figured it out. *Yes, I'll contact him right now and see if he's still happy with his job. I doubt he really is. No one likes to work for a large company when they're stuck doing all the work. All right, son. I'll talk to you later. Just so you know, you get all your brilliance from me.*

I know that. And Dad tells me the same thing when I talk to him.

She was laughing when she closed the connection. He'd thought about his mom and Marshall several times throughout the day and thought he'd make a wonderful attorney for Jamie.

Mom and Carson had been asked to come to a juvenile detention center to talk to some kids about their lives and where they were going to be in five years. Most of the kids, Mom told him, would be right back to where they had been when they were arrested, then more than likely dead within that year. But she'd seen something in Marshall that made her take one more step to make sure he didn't end up on the wrong side of a gun. She literally scared the shit out of him.

He'd been with her. Dad had been the one that was supposed to have gone with them, but he'd been called out of town. Milo had never figured out what he was supposed to be doing in protecting the women in his life. They were scarier than he'd ever been, even now. But he'd gone and watched them tell the kids the hard truth of living on the streets.

Marshall had been, like the other kids around him, popping off his mouth enough that Mom had finally gotten pissed off. Jerking the kid from the middle of his pack, she put a gun to his forehead. He just stared at her like it was an everyday occurrence to have that done to him.

"You don't scare me none. I'm gonna get out of here, and I'm going to hunt you down, lady." Mom hit him in the nose with her weapon, then handed it to him. "You want me to kill you? I can surely do that."

He put the gun to her forehead as she'd done to him. But all he did was stare at her. His buddies were telling him to pull the trigger, but Marshall just stared at her. It wasn't until later that his mom told Milo that she'd shown Marshall not only how he would die but what his mother and sister would feel when he did.

Two days after he left the facility he was in now, Marshall would have been killed with two other people in his backyard. His nephew was one of the other victims. Marshall's mother and sister would blame him and his lifestyle for the murder of the four year old and never visit his grave and would take all the pictures of him out of the house and burn them. Milo thought that would have made him hurt the most, knowing his mother would never think of him again in a good way.

"Is it loaded?" Marshall had asked his mom when he pulled the gun from her forehead. Mom took the gun from him and fired it in the air. The sound was made louder because of the echoing of the concrete walls. Not only had Marshall shit his pants, but he didn't retaliate when his buddies made fun of him. Mom then offered it back to him. "I don't want that. I don't want any of this."

Later, Mom had sat down with Marshall and told him she'd put him in a facility to get him cleaned up. He'd been about as high as she'd ever seen. That was another thing she'd taken care of, making sure there were no drugs brought in for the people trying to recover.

After graduation, Mom paid for him to go to a specialized school to catch up to his classmates he'd been with when he'd gone to school. Then at graduation, Milo's parents handed Marshall a blank check to pay for any college education he wanted to take on. He'd worked hard and gone to Harvard to become an attorney.

It was nearly five when Milo decided it was time for him to leave to go to town. He had gotten very little done, but he had made enough calls to make sure things were moving along with two of the projects he was working with for the foundation. One of them was the pantry that he and George were working on for the city.

Driving to the restaurant they were meeting at, he was happy to note that some of the shops had taken to putting out some flowers. There weren't as many places to shop in the downtown area as he was sure there used to be, as the mall opening had taken away business. But since it had closed down a few years ago, he was noticing an uptrend in little places moving back in.

The parking lot was full when he pulled in. He was glad he'd made a reservation, or he might not have been able to get a table. Just as she'd said she would, Jamie was there waiting on him. Kissing her, pulling her body as close to his as he could manage in public, she told him once again that she loved him.

"I don't think I can hear that enough. I'm going to make sure I tell you that every time I see you too." She kissed him again and told him she'd like that. As they were being shown to their table, he decided he was in the best position he'd ever been. Watching her walk was about as sexy as it got. Jamie caught him looking at her ass. "What? I like the view."

As they were seated, a bottle of champagne was brought to them, as well as a beautiful vase of violets. He was glad now that he'd called ahead and told them this was their anniversary. It was all he could think to tell them about why he wanted things to be just so for them. The restaurant had gone well above what he had expected.

"I love violets. How did you know?" He said he had his ways. When she sniffed the little purple flowers for the second time, he handed her the box he'd picked up on the way in. "What's this? I do hope you know that all this isn't necessary for you to get laid. You'd have to really screw up— Oh, those brownies! These are my new favorites, Milo. I'm guessing your mom told you I had two."

"Two? No, all she said was that you seemed to enjoy it. Actually, she told me it was like watching you have sex, but I told her I didn't want to hear that from her." They laughed and enjoyed their champagne. When their orders were taken, he was glad to see that Jamie liked her steak as he did—medium rare, with just enough pink showing to make it delicious. "I meant to ask you about the electrical issues at the hospital."

"Oh, it wasn't nearly as bad as it sounded. The faeries decided things didn't need to be plugged in to work for the place and just made everything magical." He asked her if they'd fixed it. "Not really. There is the illusion that things are plugged in, but everything works without power. I sort of like that idea in the event there is some sort of power outage. Did you know they'd gone to other hospitals to find out what was needed at this one? I thought it was a great idea for us. The better equipped we are, the bigger the likelihood that we'll be able to save a person's life."

They talked about their day. He told her about Marshall, and she said his mom had mentioned him. She told him about the insurance policy that had been located and what she wanted to do with the money. Jamie was going to donate it, whatever it was, to a college fund for high school kids to use if they qualified.

"I'm sure there are a lot of kids that would love to go to college that are on the bubble of getting financial aid. Making even a little more than the level they have planned out will keep a lot of kids from going. Even if they only need help with books or something, it will go a long way in making it so they are able to do better without the added worry." Milo agreed with her and told her they had a fund set up already. But it was for adults to use for higher education, as well as getting their high school diploma. "Great. I love that. Yes, this will help a lot of people."

Milo loved that they could have conversations, talk about things throughout their day. He knew that his parents, even though they worked together, still sat and talked about what things had come up that the other might be interested in. When they left the place, the two of them walked along the main street holding hands and eating an ice cream.

It had taken the edge off his need for her, but now that they were headed home again, his libido started to rev up. Milo wondered if they could pull over long enough for him to take her on the hood of the car. Every place he looked seemed like a good place to make love. Christ, he was going to die before they even got naked.

~*~

Once they were out of the car, Jamie couldn't stand it any longer. As soon as her door was opened by Milo, she leapt up and wrapped her legs around his hips. He said something along the lines of "Fuck yeah," but she was much too needy to care right now.

The hood of his car suffered badly for their need. She could feel the warmth of the engine through the hood. The sound and the viciousness of her panties being ripped off nearly had her coming. As soon as he was deep inside of her, Jamie came hard enough to shake the earth beneath them.

He didn't let her go as he made his way to the door. Jamie kissed him everywhere she could reach. When he dropped the keys the third time, she wanted to tell him to kick the fucking door in, but he finally got it unlocked and them inside.

Pictures fell from the wall in the entryway. Milo took her hard enough that she knew she was going to be sore but didn't care. Whatever happened to her, she knew she'd be the most loved person ever laid. Giggling a little, she was caught off guard by her next release. Her head was coming off her shoulders. She could almost feel it.

"We're not going to make it." Jamie giggled again at his tone of disappointment. "You have no idea how much I wanted to make love to you slowly. Now I can barely move, and I feel like my body has been drained of every bit of blood. And there you are, giggling at me."

"You're so handsome right now." He said that wasn't helping. "No? Well, how about if I point out that your cock is still full. That I can feel its length at the back of my throat. That I love the way you're holding me."

"No. Not helping."

He still held her to him. Each step he took, she felt her body take him just a little deeper, her breasts touching his smooth, hard chest. Jamie thought her nipples were so hard at the moment that she could have poked through a wall. When he paused on the steps to take one into his mouth, Jamie saw stars, rainbows, and dragons dancing over her head.

They didn't make it to the bedroom before they made love again. This time it was on the landing right outside their room. When Milo rolled to his back, taking her with him, he laid there for several minutes, laughing. She asked him what the hell was so funny.

"I planned this entire night with you. I have champagne right on the other side of this door. Roses all over the place, and violets as well. There is chocolate to gorge ourselves with when I made love with you, as well as a basket of fruit for us to have more energy when we're finished." He laughed again. "But we did it on every solid place on the way up here, and now, not only do I not have the strength to get into bed, but I think I'll just lay here for the rest of the night and move in a couple of days."

She joined him this time. After taking a nap, several of them, as it turned out, they were able to not just get up and go to bed, but they made love again, slowly this time. As soon as Milo spooned around her, holding her body tightly against his, Jamie closed her eyes and let sleep take her under.

Waking up with the room still dark, she wondered for a moment where she was. Sitting up on the side of the bed, she realized that Milo was gone and the bathroom light was on. She could hear him speaking, but not what he was saying. Laying back down, she straightened up the blankets as best she could before he returned to her. Jamie asked him if everything was all right.

"Yes. It was my brother Dover. He wanted to meet with me and hadn't realized it was this late. He's never been one to notice the time when he's working." Milo pulled her into his arms again. She asked him what was so important. "Oh. He thinks we need to hire more people to work directly with us. I told him Mom had said the same thing, but finding them was hard. We're having trouble finding people that can work for us that won't rob us blind. I love you. How about as soon as I can arrange it, we get married."

"All right."

When he kissed her ear then held her tightly, she laughed. This was the strangest proposal she thought had ever been done. Naked in their bed at three in the morning after making love all over the house. Laughing with him just a little, she closed her eyes and joined him in sleep.

Getting up, she knew that all that love making was the reason for her being unable to hop right out of bed. She noticed that Milo was missing again but knew too that he'd had a meeting this morning with their new attorney. She'd liked Marshall right away, and once she had him filled in on what she wanted, he sat down to work, right there in the dining room where they'd had their interview yesterday afternoon. One more thing she was going to add to her list was finding him an office.

There were boxes and crates in the hallway and in the dining room. Ignoring it for something to eat, she asked their cook what it all was. Sarah had worked for her parents at one time, and Jamie was glad she'd been willing to come back and work for her until she found someone else. She hoped Sarah would stay with her forever—the woman made the best pot roast around.

"Lady Cindi said it was some things from storage. You're to see what you want, then ask the others what they'd like. I've been told the others received such shipments and are going through theirs now." Thanking her, she looked at the food that was set in front of her. "Lord Milo said I was to make you eat. That you had a long day ahead of you, and he didn't want you fainting. What a thing to say to someone. I'm sure you have more than enough gumption to outdo him on your worst day."

"I don't know about that. I think the man is solid muscle." She did manage to eat more than half the meal and felt better for it. "Before I forget to tell you, there is some tea in a tin around here someplace that needs to be gotten rid of."

"I have done that. Who would think that putting iron in tea would make a person's blood stronger? People get stranger daily if you ask me." Sarah sat down across from her. "I'd like to hire your staff for you. I know they have to be checked out by someone, but I think I can find enough to fill out the house. The faeries are doing a bang-up job in the yard. I've never seen the gardens look so fabulous before."

"I'm sure you've seen Pem's greenhouse." She laughed and told her she'd heard the story. "Me too. Have you decided to take the cook's house in the back? It can be done in any way you wish, Sarah. Or you can live in one of the rooms here. It's entirely up to you."

"I'd like the house if you're sure you don't mind. It never got used when your parents were here. They just let us drive all the way from home even if the weather was terrible." Sarah had never been one to pull punches when it came to Jamie's parents. "Just in the few days I've been here, I can see vast improvements. It's a real pleasure to work in this kitchen, honey. It's nice when someone cares about making it easier on the people that work here rather than what it will cost."

"The place was so outdated I wasn't sure we'd ever get it up to this millennium, much less this century. But I love coming in here now. It's like a breath of fresh air." Sarah asked her about working, then asked her about her new in-laws. "You'll like them. They raised six boys, and there isn't a bad one in the lot. I think had there been, they would have taken care of it right away. Cindi is really sweet, but she has a hard side to her that scares me a little. I'm telling you this so you don't freak out a little when she does it. Milo's parents see and talk to ghosts. They're something like death something."

"The Death Watchers?" Jamie told Sarah that was it. "Oh my, really? Well, as a child, I heard of them. Not the actual names of the people, but my grandma used to tell me that when there was trouble in the other world, there was a couple of people that were called the Death Watchers that would put them in line. Is there really a white room?"

"Yes. She told me that is where they send people who cause too much trouble in both worlds. I guess there are a lot of rules the dead have to follow. And she told me that as soon as they die, all this information just appears in their minds. Like they know the rules and who the people are they're to report to." Sarah shivered and looked around the room. Jamie thought about teasing her but decided she'd not do that to her wonderful friend. "When I was overseas, I heard of them as well. Countries I've been to, they're firm believers in the dead having to follow the rules in both worlds. Going as far as to tell their kids stories about how the dead came calling and were taken away by the watchers."

"What a terrible thing to say to a child. But I guess I can understand it too. My goodness, you sure did marry into a nice big family too. Master Milo looks like one of those statues that I've seen in art shows." Jamie told her that all but Milo and George were dragons. "Dragons? You don't say. Well, if that don't beat all. You tell him if his brothers come around as one of them, I'm going to hit them with my broom. I don't need any dragons in my new kitchen."

Sarah was putting together the makings for a cake when she left her. Jamie had things to do this morning, and sitting around having fun with Sarah wasn't going to get her any closer to getting them finished. She'd forgotten how much work it was to have money. Even though she'd not spent much, it had been a lot of work just keeping it all in the right places at the right time.

Jamie was just headed to her car when her cell phone rang. It wasn't a number she knew, but she answered anyway. It took her two seconds to wish she'd just let it go to voice mail. The man was going on and on about an investment she needed to get in on the ground floor with. Finally hanging up on the man, she got into her car and drove to the hospital.

It looked like it was ready to receive patients already. There were faeries working with the builders now. The way that the little people were helping make the hospital as green as possible was going to save them a great deal of money. The entire roof on the three buildings was covered in solar panels, as was some of the parking lot. The two other buildings, one for just surgeries, had been a stroke of genius by one of the pixies that had come by. They came by a great deal just to ride the goats.

The building had generators as well as a fallout shelter in the event of tornados or other inclement weather changes. She and Pem were going to be working there when they had to operate. The third building was going to be for clinics. Not just for the people who had no insurance or very little money, but even for simple things that didn't require an emergency room visit in the middle of the night. Not only would it take some of the load off the hospital, but it would also serve as an overflow if there was a need for it. That had been George's idea.

As soon as she got out of her car, Pem met her in the parking lot, as excited as she'd ever seen her. As she gushed on about the cafeteria and how it was coming along, in between her need for breathing, Jamie told her about Sarah wanting to beat the dragons with her brooms.

It was the way they'd always been, her and Pem. Not only did they talk all over each other, but they also managed to finish each other's sentences, as well as be a great team when working together. It was as if they could read minds even back then. Dragging her to the main floor where they'd decided to put the dining area, she was seated with the cook, who was giving samples of the desserts she wished to make.

"How will you be able to make these in bulk?" The cheesecake bites were the best she'd ever eaten, and Jamie thought she could make a diet of only the apple dumplings. "I mean, I'd get sick just to eat here."

"The hospital is going to be open to the public too for a little while. We don't know yet how that will work out, but we're going to give it our best to provide meals for anyone that needs them." Pem turned to Mrs. Milner, the chef Pem had hired. "Show her how you can make this work."

With a snap of her fingers, not only was the table cleared off but there was a large moving cart filled with little bowls of the treats. She asked her what she was and was told that she was a pixie, mother to Color.

"I wanted to help out here because of the things you've done for my son and the others. They have had so much fun being able to play with the little creatures in your yard. He said you were getting a cow. I don't think they know how to contain themselves in thinking they'll be able to ride the blasted thing." Mrs. Milner laughed. "I hope you allow them to see milk come from her. I think that would have them wanting fresh milk every day. And if it gets them to drink more than just juice, I'd be so happy."

The way it was going to work was that Mrs. Milner would have only her kind working with her. It would hurt that there would be no humans or shifters getting the jobs, but if they could provide the kind of food she was telling them about, it would be better all the way around.

After they had eaten more than they should have, the two of them went to inspect the rest of the building. It would be open in a month, they were told. She thought it would be a lot sooner than that, but then she started noticing things that weren't quite finished yet. Bathrooms with no doors. There were a lot of beds that needed to be put together yet and moved. Offices needed to be set up for new staff. Even the trash company hadn't been chosen yet. Jamie wanted it done now, but she knew that rushing it wouldn't help anyone. Just thirty days, she told herself, and she'd be working with her buddy again.

Even Rachel was getting in on the excitement. She was going to help with the menus for the people on special diets. While Mrs. Milner could do that, she had no idea what it might entail.

It was nearing two when Jamie was ready to call it a day. However, she had one more thing she wanted to check on, and that was the houses at the back of their land. There was a driveway that connected the house to the back roads, so that was the way she went. They were in worse shape than the kitchen had been, and she was disgusted by how much her parents hadn't done to keep the property up. If she were able to ever talk to them again, she thought she'd be willing to give them a piece of her mind. There was no sense in leaving things to fall around your ears when there had been more than enough money to take care of things. Jamie set Jangles to work on not just getting things taken care of but also making sure the barn and the other house were livable.

Chapter 5

"The foundation is well funded, but we're still having a lot of trouble finding someone to run the thing. I know we've been doing interviews for a while now, but the fact of the matter is, no one wants to take this on that we can trust. Aunt Carson said that for every three applicants we have apply, four of them have prior records to do with not just embezzlement, but also child support issues and a lot of other shit." Milo asked his brother, Dover, how that worked, with four out of three being bad people. "I asked too, and she said that some of them were so bad she felt they needed to be counted twice. I don't know, Milo. This isn't anything I think our parents had as a problem when they were doing this."

"Because they did it all themselves until their children were old enough to help them out. Maybe we have to figure out one of us to take it on. Just until we have someone trustworthy that we can hire. I'm not saying it has to be you, but we need to see, first of all, who would like to take it on. If everyone is too busy, which I think is going to be the issue, I can do it. I wouldn't mind at all. I know that Finn has his project with the hospital. Jamie and Pem are helping him with that. George is working on the pantry projects. You're working on the school system to make sure there is funding for the kids that wish to go to college. Even Hedley is following up on projects we have working in town. As it stands right now, I'm the only one between jobs now that we're working together on everything." Dover looked so relieved that Milo had to laugh. "You could have just asked me to take over, Dover. I would have told you I could do it."

"It's not that. I just don't know how our parents did this for so long without running into trouble all the time." He told him his opinion on that. "I guess you're right. Having people investigated right from the start would have saved them a great deal of trouble. Not that they didn't have it anyway, but that was more on a personal level. What are you and Jamie doing now that you're getting settled into your home?"

"Mostly, it's been just me hanging out around the house. Jamie's been working with Finn so much that I only see her at dinnertime. I don't mind all that much, not really. I know that once the hospital is up and running, I'll see her more. So I have a lot of things I'm sort of just doing as busywork. That's why I can take on this job." Dover asked him what she and Pem had decided on with working there. "They're going to be a team. Once the hospital is complete, she's thinking she can find some of her contacts from the service to come and apply for jobs. As it stands right now, we're getting in about two hundred applications a day for nurses, kitchen staff, as well as general workers. If nothing else comes of this hospital, it sure will generate a lot of jobs for the area."

"How many of the pack has applied? I'm to understand that since they've been working in the buildings around town, Peter's had an influx of people, young shifters, coming to join his pack. He needed that more than anything." Milo told him what he'd found out. "Christ. A hundred more to his pack? Peter must but thrilled to death with that. I'm sure I would be."

"Not only that, but since he stood up to his brother, the pack seems to have taken on a better attitude toward helping out around the land. He no longer has to threaten people to get them to work." Dover said that was good. "I thought so too. By the way, I think you might already know this, but we're invited to the next pack meeting. Peter wants to introduce us to everyone so they know we can be trusted. Not only that, but also that we're the ones responsible for them having such a good year."

"This feels like a win-win for all of us." Milo agreed with his brother on that. "All right. I feel much better now that things are working in a good forward direction. I have two more things I have to take care of, and then I can take a couple of days off. I'm headed out of town to look for some shops to fill out the empty spaces in town."

After his brother left him, Milo wandered around the house and ended up in the staff's quarters on the upper level of the house. He wasn't really looking for anything in particular, but just filling out time until he had to go to the meeting he was having with his parents at their hotel. He had a hopeful feeling that they were going to move closer to them, but he wasn't sure. They had a good life at home, and they were into a lot of projects going on. Milo was afraid they were going to tell him that he needed to tell the others to start standing up on their own and stop calling them to rescue them so much. Either way, he knew he wasn't going to beg for either of them to go his way.

The first room he was in reminded him of a dorm room in older hospitals. There were still beds lined up against the walls, but the mattresses had all been removed. A little stand was between each of them. Mostly it was just a stool or something like it. Of the ten beds in the room, only one of them had a headboard. He wondered what that was about.

There were pegs above each bed, mostly just pieces of wood from a tree, but there were a couple of actual hooks. Going to the end of the room, he looked out the only window and could see the wooded area behind the house, as well as a better view of the barn.

Opening the door to the left of the window, he found a smallish kitchen. The room was devoid of anything other than a sink and a cabinet — which he thought might have been a pantry of sorts — hanging on the wall. Again, there was a view of the outside, but this one was of the driveway. He watched as a car pulled into the curved drive and parked just under the window.

He didn't rush down to see who it was but stayed at the window and watched. A stranger walked to the front of the house and disappeared. Jamie had hired a few people to work around the house just a couple of days ago, so Milo continued his looking around.

In addition to the room he was in, there was a second door across the hallway. There he found a few things. Nothing that he'd not expected, he supposed. There was a single bed in the tiny room and a few pegs on the walls, but this one had a shelf that held a couple of books. Pulling one off the shelf, he was thumbing through it when Lily came to talk to him.

"There is a man downstairs that wishes to speak to the lady of the house. He said he would speak to you if you'd see him." Milo asked her what he wanted. "While he did not say, I have read his mind, and he is here to see if you and Mistress Jamie would give him some money for a project he is trying to set up. There is no project in his mind, my lord. He believes the mistress to be as stupid as her parents were. They had given him money before without any return of it."

"So he wants to scam us the same way he did her mom and dad." She nodded, then asked what he wanted to do about it. "Tell him that the lady of the house will return at four, and he should return then. If he asks why I won't see him, tell him that—just tell him I don't work with the money or something. Just so he thinks I'm stupid too."

"That is very good. The mistress, if you don't mind me saying, will kick his bottom but hard." Milo thought the man would be lucky if he didn't get himself killed over this. "Are you thinking of redoing this room?"

"I don't know, to be honest. When the man leaves, will you come back here? I'd like to run a few things by you to see what you think." He reached out to his mom as soon as Lily left him. *Is there a way for you to reach out to Jamie's parents? I'd like a couple of answers on some things I've come across.*

I can. Right now, if you have the time. He said he did. *The mister is here. My goodness, son, I had no idea he was so badly hurt in the accident, did you?*

I don't even know what might have been the cause of the accident, to be honest. I never thought to look into it. She asked him what he needed. *There is someone here that is supposedly setting up a project and wants Jamie to give him money for it. I need to know if they remember him and if there are others they might well have given money to. Not a biggie, I guess, but it would help to be prepared for this sort of thing if it's going to be an issue.*

Milo thumbed through the book some more while he waited for his mom to get back to him. The book contained not just the names of the people that had at one time worked in the big house, but also an accounting of their wages, when they were terminated, as well as the why. Milo wondered if Jamie knew she might well have a couple of bastard relatives out there. Laughing, he put the book back and picked up the second one just as his mom got back to him, laughing.

He said his name is Mark Wheeler and that he is a good friend of the family. It's no wonder they didn't set up anything for Missy, right? They're not very good business people. Anyway, he isn't happy that his daughter is living in the house now. I don't have any idea why he'd care because he did leave it to his children. Anyway, he wants her to shut up and give the man what he needs, as he has been giving him money for years. When I asked, Booker, her father's name, couldn't think of a single time he'd either paid him back or had any kind of return on the funds going out. Milo asked if he was serious. *Oh, son, I don't think this man has any kind of sense of humor when it comes to his daughter. I think she's better off that he's not around. By the way, we have a meeting today, correct?*

Yes. I'm looking forward to it. Mom told him she was as well. *Thanks for the information, Mom. I'm going to have to look into whatever this man has taken from her family. That way, I can have a good accounting for Jamie when she meets with him later.*

I'm speaking to Carson about it now. She said she'd send what she has on this via your email. There are plenty of men and women out there like this one. Carson has been able to find about a dozen of them in the little time she's been looking. I think she's bored, to be honest with you. He laughed. Knowing that she'd been more helpful than he'd asked for, Milo thanked his mom again. *Now. What's the second thing?*

Milo told her about the books he'd found. The second one seemed to be a diary of sorts that had information about the family he didn't think was public knowledge. Just reading her a few entries from it, she seemed as intrigued as he was.

Bring it with you today — I'd like to look it over. Just because it has things in it from when I was younger and human. He laughed with her. *I love you, Milo. All my boys have been my reason for living since the day you were all brought to me as my children.*

I love you as well, Mom. So much. Every day I think of something I'd like to talk to you about, and it's so wonderful to be able to just reach out to you and talk. I never realized how much I loved that until now. She said he was making her teary. *Me too. All right. I'm going to continue to look around here, then I'm going to –*

What is it, Milo? I can feel your fear from here. He told her to wait a second. *No, I will not. Tell me what is going on.*

A ghost is here. I can see her. Mom didn't say anything, and he thought that was more frightening than seeing the ghost. *I've never been able to do that before. See ghosts. What do I do?*

Find out what she wants. He asked the woman standing before him why she was there. He knew her to be ancient simply because of her mode of dress. *Milo, you're scaring your mother. I'm going to have Winnie bring me to you.*

I'm all right. I mean, if you want to come and make sure I don't mess this up, that's good too. She's just staring at me. Mom said she was on her way. *All right. I'm all right, though. I don't know that she realizes I'm real, either.*

When she looked around the room, Milo let out a breath he'd been holding. If he was honest with himself, he wasn't as afraid as he was startled. But when she looked at him again, he knew that she knew she was dead, but not why she was there.

"I died in the early part of seventeen-eleven.

There was a winter storm that made a great many of us ill. Why are you here?" Milo told her he was the new owner of the house, with his wife. "The others, they're gone too? The younger couple with the crippled up child?"

"Yes. They're both dead. The child has been put into a nursing home for care. Do you know your name?" Mom entered the room from the doorway, and Milo could see Winnie just outside the room. She told him she was going to get Jamie if she was free. He nodded and turned to the woman again. "My mother. She's visiting from Ohio."

"I know of Ohio. It is a pretty country. I believe one of the slaves living here, or that was living here, was from there." He remembered seeing that in the book. "My name is Mildred. I was the head of the housemaids for the second floor here. There were a great many slaves here at one time, and housemaids too. How many do you have?"

"No slaves. We have people working for us, but they're free to come and go as they please. Have you figured out why you're here? I've never seen ghosts before." Mildred looked at his mom. "You know her."

"She is the Death Watcher." Mom nodded and then smiled at her. "I've done nothing wrong, my lady. I think when your son opened the book, it somehow summoned me. I have no quarrel with anyone in this house."

"Why are you here? If you were summoned here, there had to be some magic that attached you to the book. What is it you have to tell us?" Mom took the book from him and found the entry that had Mildred's name. "It says here that you died of pneumonia. It is of the same hand. How is that possible?"

"I came back to finish it. When I see one of the others pass or have children once they were beyond this place, I come back to finish their entries. It is my job, you see. To make sure the records are well kept." Mom nodded and then asked her who had done this to her. "'Tis not a hardship for me to do so. The man that owned this home during my time here, he was the one that told me, ordered me to finish the book. It was easy enough to find a witch to make sure I was to complete my job. I wish to continue to do so if the new owners have no issue with a ghost in the house."

"I don't. Do you, Milo?" He kissed Jamie when she entered the room and told her he didn't care either. "You can come and go as you please so long as you cause no one living here or the family any harm. Winnie told me you know who the Death Watcher is."

"I do, Mistress. My, but you do look like your ancestor. Your great-great grandma could have been your other half when she was alive." Mildred told them where they could find some of the old photos taken long ago. "I will return then to keep my job. If you would lay out the book so I can get to it, I can find it easily. Thank you for allowing me to do my job."

When she disappeared, Jamie and he both looked at his mom. When she burst out laughing, it was all he could do not to tell her he didn't think this was funny. Jamie, however, didn't have any trouble asking.

"You two. You're able to talk to ghosts. I think it's wonderful." Jamie said she didn't. "Well, it's a bit late for that now, I guess. Welcome to the Ghost Watcher family, my dears. I'm so glad to have you aboard."

~*~

The pictures had simply shown up on the dining room table about an hour before they were to meet his parents in town. He told his mom what they had, and plans were changed for them to come to the house. Mom loved old photographs as much as his dad did. They were still going over the first book of them when Sarah told them that dinner was ready. It was nothing more than hot shots, his all-time favorite meal of beef and gravy over slices of bread and mashed potatoes. However, none of them wanted to stop looking at the pictures. Then Mom found the picture of Jamie's great-great-grandmother.

"Good heavens, you do look like her." Holding up the picture, an old tin-type photo, so that everyone could see it, Milo was amazed. They didn't just look alike, but the two of them could have been identical twins. From the way they both wore their hair pulled back in a long braid to them being built the same. "She's a very lovely woman, your grandmother."

"She looks so young here. I would love to have been able to meet her. Can you imagine the stories she'd have about this house before it was upgraded and added onto?" Mom laughed, and Jamie looked at her. "What? You'd not like to talk to your ancestors?"

"I have, as a matter of fact. They're wonderful people. At least some of them were. Turn around, Jamie. I think you're stronger than I first thought." Jamie didn't move except to look at him. He turned and saw her. "Jamie, I do believe your grandmother is waiting on you to acknowledge her."

Jamie did turn then. She did so slowly and looked at the woman standing just inside the doorway to the dining room. Her smile, so much like Jamie's, could have lit up the sky. But she only had eyes for one person. Jamie.

"Hello, child. My, but you're as beautiful as Mildred said you were. Just look at you." Jamie stood up, and Milo realized they were the same height as well. "Eat your dinner, and I will tell you what I'm able. I'm hoping that the Death Watchers will allow me a little bit of leeway on this. I might well forget myself at times and tell too much."

"You tell her what you know, Nelly. I do believe there are things you know that would help them both.

This is my son, Milo Manning." Nelly looked at him but turned back to his mom. "It's all right. I won't hold anything against you. This I swear to you as the Death Watcher."

"Even the treasures she can use?" Mom looked at Dad, and when he nodded, Mom told Nelly it would go a long way in helping others, so for her to tell all. "Thank you, my lady. I have heard you were the best of the Watchers. You've no idea how long I've watched over this house and kept others away from it. They would have squandered it, you know. Used it for things that would not have helped even those that found it."

Dinner was served by the faeries, and as they ate, Nelly looked around the room. She told them of the things that had been added to this room and what it had been when the house had been built. The room they were in now had been a parlor, a room to receive guests when they came calling.

"Back in the day, we had many visitors to this estate. Most of them were nothing more than gawkers, as you can imagine. They wanted to see how we lived. We had a great deal more things than them, but nothing like they did in the way of love. My husband, he was a good man, but he wasn't very loving." Milo asked her about the name Darkhouse. "Oh my, that is a funny one. The stories I've heard of our name would just make you wonder at what people were thinking."

"You're not Darkhouse then?" Nelly shook her head at Jamie as she sat down at the table with them. "You know, when I was looking through some of the pictures, I could see that the house was dark. I'm thinking that is where the name came from."

"'Tis right. We were the Darks. The house, as you've seen there in the picture, was very dark at the time it was built. No brick back then, though we could have had it, but stone, right up from the river, was used to put this place together. We were the Darks, who lived in the dark house on the seventh street from the jail. Things like that seemed to stick, I guess. Go on now, eat your supper. 'Tis getting chilled."

Jamie ate then but still peppered Nelly with questions. She had a few of her own, mostly about how the house was suiting them. It was a strangely put question, but Jamie told her now that she'd had it suited to the two of them, it was much homier.

"That it is. I know your parents. My descendants, I guess you'd call them. Not at all the kind of people I would have liked to claim. Cold people, as I'm sure you know. They wished to have a sit down with you. I'd do it just so they can get whatever it is out of their bonnets, but I'd not take anything they say to you to heart. You're a good woman, Jamie, and you'd be better off not allowing them any say so in your life and how you live it." Jamie told her she wasn't going to allow anyone to dictate her life anymore. Not that they ever did, she told her grandmother. Then she reached over and took Milo's hand into hers. "I'm a woman in love with the greatest family a person could hope for. They've made me see, without any extra effort on their parts, what a truly loving family can be. My parents can stick their opinions up their asses for all I care."

Her laughter rang through the room. Nelly didn't laugh like a dainty person but hooted loudly and with all her heart. It was a good sound, Milo thought. A sound that had been greatly missed in this house when Jamie's parents had been living.

After they were all finished, Nelly showed them around the house, indicative of the time that she had lived here. There were places she didn't understand until she was in the next room, but overall, the house didn't look anything, other than the front entrance, like it had when the house was used in her time. Nelly and her family were the third generations that had lived and raised families in the house.

However, once they were outside, it was as if a whole new world had been opened for them. She told them of the gardens that had been put in. The type of foods they'd grown. Milo found himself recording the other woman just so he would be able to tell his brothers. It wasn't until about five minutes after he'd gotten his phone out that his mother pointed out that she was a ghost, therefore not recordable, and he began making notes in a little notebook he'd picked up in his office.

"Over there, we had us some pigs. Used their droppings for the roses that were around the fencing. Kept the varmints out, I tell you. But also kept the kids out. That was something we'd not planned on, but it worked for us." Milo asked her about a barn. "Oh sure, we had a nice sized one out there from the house. About the place you have that one now. Some of it is built on the property the old one was on. I think you might well like the things you find in it. But we have to go to the place you're using for a wine cellar. It's where we're headed now, if you do not mind too much. So you know, young man, I'm glad you don't partake of the evil swill like the miss's ancestors did." He said his momma would hurt him. "She's a good person. You don't ever forget that."

"I won't."

The basement was a combination of all kinds of floorings and walls. The wine cellar that Nelly had mentioned had not just a stone floor, but walls and the ceiling were also stone. Dad pointed out that the ceiling as well as the inside wall was newer stone but was very old as well. Milo was going to have his uncle come over and touch the walls to see what sort of story they had to tell. He'd bet anything there wasn't a joist or board in this house that didn't have something to say.

There were only a few wines and other bottles on the well-made racks. About a couple of dozen, he thought. Dad told him that, judging by the dates on them, they might be worth some money unless he wanted to keep them as something special. He had an idea running in his head, but he kept it to himself.

Milo would bet that whoever had put the racks in had been a wine enthusiast and had filled the beautifully oak racks fully. The grid, he thought it was called, would have held at least a hundred bottles on each side, while the other two walls held only about half that. He and his dad pulled the racks out carefully and set them aside, the well-wrapped bottles as well.

After they were removed, they decided to wait until tomorrow to start on the floor. Nelly had to rest anyway, and he was sure the rest of them were as tired. His parents said they'd stay with them, and he was in his room with Jamie when he remembered they'd not spoken with his parents about what they'd wanted.

Tomorrow, he told himself. They'd make sure they had to sit and talk tomorrow. He was also going to invite his brothers over, along with the wives, for dinner. It would be nice if his parents were leaving and not returning to have a good meal. Or if they were staying, they would make a good celebration meal instead.

"I wanted to ask you something. I wanted to

ask you earlier this morning, but you kept distracting me." Milo wiggled his brows at Jamie as he stripped down to his skin. "See, you're doing it again. Stop that."

"What? I'm just being me. My humble, lovable self." She snorted, and he laughed. "What is it you wanted to talk to me about, love? Whatever it is you want, I will make sure it's yours. You want everything I have? You already have that."

"That was very sweet. But I want you to marry me as soon as possible. I know we've talked a little about it before, but I don't think you thought I was serious." He stopped still and stared at her. "Or not. But I think marrying you would be everything I want. No, that's not right. It would be everything I'd ever want until we have a child. You did say you'd like to have a child with me, right, Milo? If we can?"

"Yes. As many as you would give me." He got into bed with her and pulled her to his body. "Love? You do know that I would marry you right this moment if it were possible."

She pulled away and turned to look at him. "Good. But tomorrow will be perfect. Your parents will be here, and you'll need to invite your brothers and their wives too. I've already contacted your aunt Carson, who I think is scary, by the way, and she is getting us a quicky license. Actually, she has had it filed already and said that your father could marry the two of us." He kissed her, feeling all the love he had for this woman surround his heart tightly. Looking at her after she told him she loved him as well, he pulled her even closer than he had before. "Then, however we need to do this, I'd like to have a dozen or so children with you. Although not all at one time. Just one at a time if you can manage that."

"I'll try. But don't blame me if you have more." She said she'd never do that to him. "I love you, Jamie. You're the best friend and wife that a man like me could have ever hoped for."

"Ditto." He grinned when he closed his eyes. For as much as he wanted to make love to her, he was going to wait. Tomorrow they would officially be man and wife because his dad would say so. "By the way, your mother is going to be my maid of honor. Pem suggested it so that it would be a major family event. Now, go to sleep. We have a big day tomorrow."

Yes, he thought, he was the luckiest man on earth.

Chapter 6

"What do you think?" Pem stared at her, and Jamie had a feeling she thought she was stupid. "I can still change if you think this is just silly. I just thought that—"

"You are, simply put, beautiful. I didn't know you were planning on doing this, but I think you got it perfect. It's a wedding dress that is more than just timeless in its beauty, but it is timeless in that it was your great something grandmother's. The faeries did such a wonderful job in replicating it for you. Did your grandma see it?" Jamie told her she had and had to leave. "No wonder. I bet she was so moved by emotion that she didn't know what to say to you. This is the most wonderful thing you could have done, you know?"

"Well, at the time, it seemed like a good idea.

Like having Cindi as my maid of honor and you giving me away. But now that I'm thinking about it, I might have just been too sentimental. I'm not usually like this." Pem told her that was what made it so wonderful. "I hope so. If Milo decides not to marry me today, not that I think he will, but I'm going to put it all on you. Just so I can have a romantic honeymoon."

"I'll take it. Because I don't think he's going to be upset at all." Jamie hoped so. This was so important to her. She wasn't entirely sure why, but it was, so she went with it. "By the way, I think you having Xavier do the deed is making Finn and Theo jealous. I don't know about you, but I get a kick out of them being jealous of one another. Saying that women are catty isn't anything compared to what these guys are at things. I'm betting the other three have their dad do it as well."

"He'd love it. When I asked him about it, he was so teary that I hugged him. You know me—I'm not much of a hugger—but it felt right to have him hugging me." She grinned at her friend. "I think, seeing how happy their father is right now, he'll be a mess on those days. I mean, I'm just his daughter-in-law. The boys asking will be epic."

Cindi joined them a few minutes later. She stood in the doorway to their bedroom and sobbed about how beautiful Jamie looked. Jamie thought if she could get half that reaction from Milo, she'd be happy. After getting major hugs from her, they were all set.

The flowers were from their faeries. The dress had been made by them as well. She'd been surprised by Jangles suggesting that they could whip it up for her. Also, and this touched her in ways she couldn't put a word to, that Winnie had provided them with an island all to themselves, and she was going to take them there and pick them up. That way, they could get there and get back quickly and not have to worry about planes and ships taking them out to it.

"Are you ready?" She was and watched as Cindi started for the door. When she turned back and hugged her again, it was difficult for Jamie to control her emotions. "I love you, Jamie. I love you and all the girls so much. Thank you for doing this for us."

She wasn't sure if she meant having them as a part of the wedding or marrying her son. Whatever it was, Jamie was thrilled she could do it for her. As soon as Cindi was out the door, Jamie let out a long breath and took hold of Pem's arm.

The house was perfect for a wedding. Not only did it support a large dining room, thanks mostly to the faeries, but it also had the most beautiful staircase that curved around and ended up in a large receiving area. When she paused on the steps to look at Milo, she could see on his face that he was pleased with her choice of dress.

"I told you so." Pem kissed her on the cheek as they descended the rest of the stairs. As they were walking to the living room, which had been emptied of all the furniture for this, Pem spoke to her again. "You're my best friend in the entire world, Jamie. And I couldn't think of a better way for us to be related than you marrying Milo. I love you."

Before she could say anything, even if she could have spoken around the lump in her heart, Pem was seated. Then she hopped up as if she'd only just realized she was supposed to hand her off to Milo. Taking both their hands into hers, Pem addressed them and the few guests that were there today.

"Milo, I'm giving you my best friend today. I love you both very much. However, I want to say this to you both. If either of you gets hurt by the other, there will be no hole deep enough that I won't find you and kick your fucking asses. Do I make myself clear?" Everyone laughed a little, but she was sure they all realized that Pem wasn't joking. They both nodded at her. "Good. Just so you know, I want you to make me an aunt as soon as possible. And I'm going to spoil the shit out of it too. Welcome to the Manning family, Jamie. And you, Milo, are one of my favorite brothers-in-law."

When she sat down, Jamie looked at Milo and burst out laughing. The look on his face as he stared at Pem was priceless. And when Rachel did the sign that she was watching him, he shivered. Laughing a little had Milo turning to her.

"I would never hurt you." She kissed him on the mouth and told him she knew that. "You're my life. Everything. You know that, don't you?"

"I do." He asked her then to explain that to her sisters. "I will. After you say, I do. Then we can be on our honeymoon and perhaps never return."

"Yeah. I like that." He kissed her then, and it took his dad clearing his throat for him to pull back. "Dad, I have the best of the best here. It's hard to resist her."

"Give it your best shot, son. We have a cake to eat yet." Jamie had forgotten that Xavier loved cake. Mostly it was the frosting, but he got around to eating the other part too. "Come on now. Let us get the two of you married and celebrate."

They were married in less time than she thought went into planning the wedding. After they kissed for the first time as man and wife, each of his brothers kissed her on the cheek, then hugged their brother. The women, all of them good friends now, hugged her and kissed her as well. She had a family now, and one she was very happy to be a part of.

The cake was delicious, as was the rest of the food. Sarah and the faeries had gone all-out, making this a special day, and she was glad they had helped. Just as she was going to the dining room for more treats, the doorbell rang, and Milo answered it.

The pack had shown up to give them wedding gifts, it seemed. She was so touched by the small gifts the children and adults gave them that she invited them for food and cake. The children were especially delighted, and the adults were happy to see Xavier and Cindi, as well as the rest of the Mannings. She'd not even known they had met before today. She asked Cindi about it.

"We have contacts all over the world. Mostly it's through one channel or another that leads us to them, but we do have some pretty important people on our list. They can move things around so we don't have to go through as much red tape as it normally would take." She asked if the hospital was one of them. "In a way. We don't do things that would cause harm to anyone else, but this was something that was greatly needed, and moving through the red tape would have cost more time than we thought was necessary. So, they just hurried things along for us."

"I'm glad. I've heard that we're getting applicants out the ass for this. A lot of them knew that if the Mannings were involved, it would be a good project, or job in this case, to be a part of. It must be nice to have that much goodwill from people." Cindi pointed out that she, too, had that sort of goodwill. "I do, I guess. But I'm just happy to be Milo's wife."

With another hug, Cindi laughed. "We're

happy to have you as Milo's wife as well, my dear. You're good for him. And the rest of them. When I saw what the other two did to him at the ceremony, I nearly laughed out loud. My goodness, you've gotten close to all of us in a very short amount of time."

"Pem and I have been friends since our days in the service. But Rachel seemed to fit right in with us too." They were walking around the backyard now — the house was quite full, it seemed. "We're going to have someone come out and find the graves at the end of the property. I guess there are a lot of places around here that have graves from big houses. We're going to see what we can find out about them." Cindi told her that Milo had told her that. "He's going to write a book about this house. Not that he cares if it's a bestseller or not, but he's getting insider information that will really make it true."

"He'd not mentioned that to me. I think that's a wonderful idea. Milo and the boys have done just about everything, but Milo seemed to excel at writing. There was a time when I think he wrote several children's books and illustrated them. I'll have to look for them for you. I have the originals for each of them." Jamie asked if she wanted to keep them. "No. I'm handing them off to a person I know will take care of them. And you'll enjoy reading them to your children, I believe."

"We're going to have children if we can. I guess

we're still trying to figure things like that out." Cindi said it was mostly trial and error on things they were able to do. "That's what Rachel told me. She said she and Finn wouldn't be able to have children, they didn't think. That's so sad for them. But they're going to try and adopt as many children as they can."

"If you're worried that we won't love them as much as we would biological grandchildren, I want to point out that neither Milo nor George is ours." Jamie told her it never entered her mind. "Good. I didn't want you to think I was going to be a terrible grandmother."

"Never. I know you and Xavier will be the best grandparents. I'm hoping you'll spoil them and love them as much as you possibly can." Jamie looked at her mother-in-law. "In order to do that, however, I'm thinking you'll need to purchase a home here and live near your children. I know for a fact that is what Milo is hoping you'll do."

"We thought about it a great deal, to be honest with you. While we do have businesses at home, they're not as fun as helping my boys with their projects." Jamie asked her if they were moving. "Yes. We've already found a house to live in. We're going to live in the one Milo gave up to live here, which, I'm telling you right now, I'm sorely jealous about. This is a home that will have memories forever, I'm thinking."

"Not all of them good ones, but the bad ones are fading quickly now. I want to see my children playing in the backyard with the animals and faeries. Having them have sleepovers." Cindi asked her if those were the things she'd done. "No. I wasn't really a kid that had much in the way of friends. Mostly because of my parents. I know that now. I thought it was just me being the odd kid out, but I've come to realize it was because they were so odd. They never went to school functions. They didn't even go to my graduation, citing that they had more important things to do. Which is exactly what they told me. After a while, I just didn't mention anything to them and moved out as soon as I was able. I think they wouldn't have put up a fuss if I'd moved out even earlier, so long as I wasn't bothering them."

"I would like to say that wasn't true, but I've spoken to them on several occasions. They wish to speak to you. Mostly I think it's to tell you how disappointed they are in what you've done. But then, I do believe you're strong enough to know what you've accomplished is well beyond anything they did with their lives, and they should move on." She asked her if she'd send them to the white room. "No. Not yet, at any rate. They're only annoying to me, and I think that is because of the relationship you and I have. I want to smack them around, to be honest with you."

"Can you do that?"

Cindi laughed as they entered the house again. Jamie loved this woman and thought she'd have been a wonderful mother to her. But then, she'd not have been able to marry Milo, and that was much more important than having a good mom. Besides, she thought to herself, her parents had made her what she was today, and that was what she needed right now.

Winnie found them once things started to die down around the house. Most of the guests had left, but her new family had stuck around. They were going to clean up after they left for the island. It never occurred to her to ask Winnie how she was going to take them both, and when she took their hands, and they were suddenly there, Jamie squealed in delight. It was much nicer than she could have imagined.

Then they were alone. In the middle of a large sea with nothing more than their wits to entertain themselves. She was going to entertain the fuck out of Milo.

~*~

Milo watched Jamie sleep. She'd worn the two of them out so much last night after they'd had supper that he was sure they'd sleep the day away. Today they were going to go swimming, and then try and catch their food. If that didn't work out for them, Winnie had told them there was a faerie on the island just for them, and all they had to do was call for him. Benji was enjoying the fruits of the island while he was there as well.

"You should know I can tell when you're awake. While you don't snore all that loudly, you do it on occasion." Jamie turned toward him and smiled. "Good morning, husband of mine."

"I do not snore, and hello, my wife." He felt sappy when he said that, knowing full well he did indeed snore. But kissing Jamie on her back, he watched her stretch. "Are you hungry? Benji was by earlier and told me he brought us some fruit to have with our breakfast. I'm not sure what he considers fruit here, but there are some very pretty shells on the platter as well. Want to get up or eat later?"

"Now. I'm starving. I only just realized." When she stood up and stretched again, he had to bite his tongue rather than beg her to come back to bed with him. "I can feel your hard-on all the way over here. How about we have a shower together and — I wasn't finished, Milo."

He'd leapt from the bed so quickly she laughed at him. "I know, but you're pushing all the right buttons for me to take you again. By the way, I've been warned that making love on the beach isn't all that romantic. There is just too much sand getting into places it shouldn't be."

When she laughed, heading to the shower, he followed her. Since he'd had one earlier, he sat on the toilet and talked to her. There was plenty enough going on without him trying to make love to her while she was showering. When the water was turned off, he headed to the kitchen to make them something to eat. Aunt Winnie was standing in the kitchen.

Don't speak. He nodded and looked around. *I want you to go to the water's edge and wait for Hudson. He's going to take you —*

Not without Jamie. She looked pissed but then nodded at him. *Can you tell me what's going on? What is coming for us?*

Not you, but Jamie. And it's too complicated right now. Please, do just what I tell you. He promised her he would so long as Jamie was safe. *I'm going to go and get her. You don't move, Milo. Not that you can die, but they'll harm you in a way that you'll regret being alive. All right?*

When he nodded, his aunt disappeared. As soon as she was gone, he could hear the sound of people moving along the outside of the house. There were sounds he didn't know as well. When something broke just behind him, Uncle Hudson appeared and wrapped him in his arm. He was at his home just as Winnie appeared with Jamie in her arms. Then both his aunt and uncle disappeared, and they were left standing in their living room. Mom came out of the kitchen and hugged them both. Milo asked her what was going on.

"It's terrible. Jamie, your parents have taken out a contract on you and Milo. They've been able to tell someone where you are and that you're worth a great deal of money. They were to take you out to the middle of the ocean and drop you in it. Both of you. While you'd live forever, you'd not be found for perhaps centuries. The waters are too vast, and finding you the way they were to drop you would have not had you touching the earth." He asked his mom how they were to do that. "Tie you both to blocks of concrete with ropes, and drop you over the boat they came in. I'm sorry. So sorry about this."

"I know what we are to you." Mom nodded at Jamie. "We're to assist you with the dead. We're going to end them. All manner of the dead that causes trouble."

He didn't understand. Milo wanted to ask what Jamie meant, but Uncle Hudson returned and smiled at them both. Not sure how to understand the smile, he asked him if his aunt was all right.

"Yes. The men are being brought before Cooper. He's taking care that they have a good understanding of how not to treat a dragon when he's a nephew of the king. I don't think they'll be long for this world." Milo started to point out he wasn't a dragon when his uncle put up his hand. "You are. You're the son of a dragon, which carries as much weight as any one of us would. Cooper is about as pissed off as I've ever seen him. And Christ, don't get me started on Carson. She was ready to have them all burnt without a trial."

They waited on Winnie to return. When she did, she sat down and asked for a glass of juice and smiled at them both. She didn't look the least bit happy or cheerful, and he was sure she knew that. Instead of explaining what was going on, she looked at Jamie.

"You've figured it out, haven't you?" Jamie said she had, but not all of it. "I'll help where I can, but I think once you start thinking about it, you'll see that the two of you are the perfect choice in this. Milo is strong-willed, and you're both smart. I never thought of the need for the dead to be destroyed, but now that I've done some research on it, I can see where it would be very helpful to both worlds."

"How do you kill the dead? That seems redundant if you ask me." Jamie said it was destroy, not kill. "I don't understand the difference. How do you destroy someone that isn't living in the first place?"

"Do you remember Stanley and David? Nephews of Pem?" Milo said he did, but Jamie had to be filled in on the story. Mom explained the way they were sent to the white room.

"So they're there. In their own section of the rooms. Are you telling me that it's not enough?"

"No. Not just them, but Caroline, their mother too. They're poison, you see. Their anger is seeping through the walls and into the world there. Not that they can reach one another, but it's still being poisoned with their anger — their evilness, I guess you could call it. They need to be erased, I guess, is a better word for them. The same with Jamie's parents. What they did with trying to have you killed is against all laws. And while I can send them away, with the poison that is already there, I fear it will be only a matter of time until it's no longer going to hold them. There isn't any telling what sort of monstrous creatures will be able to come through once they figure out that the rooms are nothing more than a place in their mind. They're all there together, in this place, without the ability to see or speak to one another. Because they simply do not have any idea where they are."

"So what you're telling me is this white room, it's nothing more than something that you've planted into their minds that makes them think they're alone and without sound." His mom nodded at Milo. "I thought for sure it was a place, but I did wonder when you filled it, where you were to put ghosts after that."

"To be honest with you, son, we both thought it was a place. As part of the magic we got, nowhere was it explained until we realized that there was trouble brewing. Then when we got more information on it, we realized the problem was part of us sending them along. The magic we give them when they're not for this world." Milo asked his dad what they were going to do now. "I'm not entirely sure how it works, but you and Jamie will destroy the people that are even now causing us trouble. Such as Stanley and David and your parents, Jamie."

"All right. We'll do it. But I want to talk to them first. Will that be all right?" Milo looked at Jamie and asked her if she'd heard them about her parents. "I did. I know them well enough to know they're nothing but troublemakers. When I think about growing up, they were forever doing things to stir shit up until there were fights all over the town. Once, when I was about eight, they got into it with the paperboy. While that sounds harmless enough, they got the boy fired, and his parents lost their jobs as well. Not only that, but the people had to move away without a forwarding address because they had been blamed for things that were not their doing. My parents thought it was funny."

They were to call them forth, but Jamie asked for time to gather some information. Milo asked to help her, and she agreed. He had no idea what sort of information she'd need to settle up with the dead, much less her parents, but he was willing to help in any way he could.

"By the way, we're moving into your old house, Milo." He stared at his parents for several seconds before he got up and pulled them into his arms. "We weren't sure you'd want us to. Not with you being newly married, and the other two practically newlyweds as well. But we want to be close for grandchildren. You six are the first to move away, and we wanted to be with you through this time in your life. We'll not be a bother."

"Yes, you will, and I will love every second of it." They laughed with Jamie as she continued. "I need to be a good mom, and I can't think of better people than the two of you to help me with that. Even if we're only to have human children, they still will need the very best in the way of grandparents."

"Thank you for that."

As they parted ways, Milo had to think that he was getting off easy here. He didn't know what was in store for them as destroyers of the dead, but he was sure it wouldn't be as easy as he could think it would be.

Just as he was sitting down to begin working on the foundation paperwork, Nelly joined him.

"Is it true that you're going to be writing a book, young man?" He asked her if that would be all right with her. "So long as you don't try and make us out to be more than we are. You will need to write the truth, not some trumped-up version of what you think will sell. Does that matter to you? That it sells?"

"No. Like you said, I want the truth out there. I can't think of a better way of getting it out there than with you and the others telling it to me. I think a great many people will be entertained with just the name of Darkhouse and how it came about. Not to mention all the treasures we're hoping to unearth in the sublevels here. We never did get back to that."

"You will. I'm not sure when, but I have no doubt you will. There are a great many treasures, as you call them, down there. Not like money, but some things that will be of great value all the same." He asked her if any of it would be show worthy, as in putting it in a museum. "Oh, I would think so. Especially since the Darks were the first family here. Did you know that? We traveled very far to come here and settle. It was a good place for the first family to come. I think you would be well served to talk to all of them, the generations from the start. While a lot of them didn't live in the house back then, there were lean-tos that they used as their makeshift homes until this house was finished."

"I'd like that. Very much so. Do you know them?" She said she did and that their names were in the big Bible that he'd find too. "That would be a treasure, I think. To be able to show it off. Much like the book that Dawn cares for. I think people would be interested in something like that."

"I do believe there are records that you can find. We would hide away things like the Bible and other things that meant a great deal to us so they'd not be stolen. Sometimes they'd be gotten by varmints, but we learned ways of keeping them away over the decades. I have noticed that there are no such creatures around now that you're living here. I think it has to do with all the magic you have, as well as having dragons around a great deal. You're good for such things."

He wasn't sure if she was insulting him or not, so he didn't comment. When her laughter rang through the room he was in, Milo had to smile. He was going to write this book for her. And when it was finished, he was going to dedicate it to her laughter. The sound of it should be bottled, he thought, for all the sadness in the world. It was, he thought, as contagious as a child's laughter or even that of a baby. He found it impossible to feel bad after hearing any of them.

Finding all the pictures that Nelly had told them about made things easier to date. While there were not a lot of names on the back of some of them, Nelly and a couple of other ghosts were able to help with that. Some of them even remembered years that they'd been born and died, but nothing more about their lives. He was able to put together a good line of their tree by the time supper was called. When Jamie joined him, he asked her how her research was going.

"Remind me never to try and hide anything from your family. They have an ability to find things that are scary." He laughed when she did. "I've been able to get everything I need, and then some. I'm pleased with the information, don't get me wrong, but my parents were not nice people. Nor were those kids. I'm thinking they should have been in some sort of special place since the day they learned to walk. They were just plain evil."

"I know. I've heard some of the things they'd done around their neighborhood that frankly make me sick. The fact that they planned on killing Pem and her grandma makes me want to find them and make them pay over again. But we'll take care of them. Right?" She smiled and nodded at him. "What's with the smile? I have a feeling I'm missing something."

"You are, but through no fault of your own. I'm going to have your baby."

Milo watched as she walked into the other room. He was still sitting there when Lily told him to close his mouth and to find his mate. She was waiting on him. Christ. He was going to be a father? Needing to hold onto Jamie, he found her at the dining room table, laughing, eating a large salad for her meal. Picking her up, he swung her around the room and sat her down.

"Did I hurt you?" She smacked him on the chest. "Are you sure? A baby? Who told you? I'm assuming it was one of my relatives. Who was it?"

"No, you didn't hurt me. Yes, I'm sure. Yes, usually, women have babies no matter what they are. Winnie told me. And yes, I do believe she is a relative of yours." Jamie kissed him on the mouth. "I love you, Milo Manning."

"And I love you, Jamie Manning." He held her tightly, then hugged her again. There was a great deal to talk about, he supposed, but for now, he was thrilled that he was going to be a dad. "Good lord, I'm going to be a father."

She was still laughing when he had to sit down. Milo wasn't going to retaliate because she was with child. Deciding he'd not call her that, he sat down and watched her eat, very careful not to encourage her to eat more or to drink a lot of juice. He might be a first-time father, but he was far from stupid.

Chapter 7

Imp didn't move when they were all told to sit on the floor with their hands on their heads. She wasn't going to do anything until the time was right. Knowing that the three men and a woman were robbing the bank on a Friday morning told her they were stupid anyway. Only a numb-nuts would rob a bank that early in the morning after all the money had been put in the armored truck and sent out.

"Who's in charge?" She supposed she could have pointed out it was the dead man on the floor of his office, but she kept her mouth shut. "I asked a question, and I want you to answer."

Imp wondered why he thought the lady wearing her slippers and a hairnet would be working in the bank. She was the elderly lady that came in once a day to check on the balance of her account. And every day, Imp or one of the other tellers working there would tell her there was nothing in the account that she'd have to wait for her social security check to hit. There were five or so bucks in the account, but they never told her that. Mrs. Shelby would take that, and the account would be closed. She'd not get her checks at all if she did that.

Working here was a good way to make some money. Usually, there wasn't any kind of stress. But Imp had no desire to get shot up when she had more important things to do today. Like breathing and having all her blood stay where it was.

"You. Do you work here?" The lady sitting next to her on the floor, Mary Roberts, shook her head. She did, as a matter of fact, work right beside Imp, but when she turned to her, telling the man Imp worked there, Imp thought about never working for her again. If it was to come up after this, she reminded herself. "I want you to get me the manager."

"You already killed him. And if you're going to ask me to open the safe, I can't do that either. You killed the only person that can do that for you." He put the gun at her forehead. "You kill me, and that will definitely not get you any answers. I don't know the combination any more than you do. They don't let us have it as part-timers."

"Why?" She waited for him to say why what, but when he didn't, she finally had to ask him. "Why don't they give it to part-timers? Don't they think people want something out of the vaulter when they come in?"

That was the third time he'd called it a vaulter like it was some gymnastic jump or something. Instead of correcting him, she told him what she knew. That they didn't want anyone that wasn't full-time knowing the combination in the event of the bank being robbed.

"That's just stupid." She didn't tell him she thought robbing the bank was stupid, but he seemed to not care what her opinion was. So when he got up to pace, she didn't move. It was becoming harder and harder to sit still. Imp had been on her way to the bathroom when the people had shown up. Now she really had to pee. "We had this place all ready to be robbed, and now it's not going the way we want."

Again, she had plenty to say to that but prudently kept her mouth shut. Turning to her again, he asked her what was in the drawers they were to use.

"Nothing. I mean, you came in right before we were to open and killed the bank manager right away. He hadn't gotten out the drawers we were to use." Imp nearly screamed when someone spoke to her right by her ear. "Who is that?"

"I'm not going to tell you my name, you moron." She nodded at the man, hoping the woman who had spoken would understand that she meant her. The woman spoke again.

You have the power to end this. Why haven't you? Imp asked her what she was talking about, knowing full well what she could do. *You are very powerful, Imp Perkins. Just stomp your foot, and the police will come in and gather up the idiots. They are, too, as you've noticed.*

I just got my life together here, and I'm not going to do something to jeopardize that. I don't know what people will think if I suddenly just make everyone within a mile fall on their asses. It'll come back to bite me in the ass, and I think you know that, whoever you are, as well as I do. The laughter had her smiling. It was just like what she thought the word mirth would sound like if the dictionary had sound. *You should know if you're aware of me, that I'm not going to cause trouble when I don't have to.*

He's going to kill everyone in that bank. Can you live with that? She told the voice that she could. *No you can't. You have a tender heart, and you'd hate for anyone to be hurt. That's why you ran here a few months ago.*

If you know so much, why the hell don't you fix this? I'm assuming you're as capable as I am. She told her she was, but wasn't allowed to interfere with humans. *And what makes you think I can? Answer me that? Maybe I can't either.*

Ah, but you can. Do you know why? Because I know just what you are. Imp wasn't sure she was telling her the truth or not. She had no idea what she was or the power that she could wield. *If you do this for me, I'll not only tell you what you are but also where you're from. That would be worth it, right?*

I don't like you very much right now. She told her who she was. *Well, Winnie Manning, not only do I not like you, but I don't care for your name, either. I'm reasonably sure you're not related to the dragons by the same name. Sounds petty, I know, but my mother's name was Winnie, and she was a fucking cunt.*

Standing up, she was told to sit down. Instead of following orders, she touched the man with her fingertips and said, "Freeze." He looked, for all appearances, just like a man standing still. However, every organ in his body, including his heart, was frozen solid.

Taking his gun from his fingers, she shoved him to the floor. Turning to the other people that had been sitting in the bank with her, she told them to go to the bathroom. However, they just sat there.

"Get your asses in the bathroom before the next guy comes out here and starts firing at you." They moved then. The three other tellers were moving quickly, and she closed her eyes. "Christ, they'll hire anyone."

Winnie laughed but didn't say anything until she was headed toward where the vault was. *There is a man to your right. He's looking toward where you're coming from. When I tell you, you can move.* She waited, and when Winnie said now, she came around the corner and fired twice, hitting him in the head both times. *Good shot. The other two men are in the backroom trying to find the combination to the vault. They don't have any idea that you killed the other man. They're making enough noise to wake the dead in there.*

Entering the room, she was shot once in the shoulder as soon as she fired on the first man. Killing the second man, she sat down on the floor and tried to work her way through the pain. Winnie asked her if she was all right.

Sure. Getting shot like this is an everyday occurrence for me. You said you'd tell me what I am. What the fuck am I, and how much longer do you suppose I'll live? I've seen enough for several lifetimes. Hell, I've seen several lifetimes. Coughing, a little blood appearing on her fingers, she thought about putting the gun to her head and knew it would only hurt. Nothing would kill her. *Tell me or not. Right now, I'm out of here.*

I'm afraid that's not possible. Imp asked her what she was talking about. *You leaving there. I mean, you could try, but they'll hunt you down. The police already think this is an inside job. If you flee, they'll put out an all-points for you, and since there are four dead men that you killed, they'll blame you for that too. It sucks to be immortal and have a couple of life sentences.*

Did you fucking know this before? She said she

hadn't, but she could see it playing out that way. Imp heard a noise behind her and put her hands up when she was told to. *Right now, I could gladly hunt you down and murder you.*

You can't, I'm afraid. I'm an immortal as well. And as for your comment earlier, I am a part of the Manning dragons. I'm their protector. She asked her again what she was. *You're an elemental fae. You can also use fire should you wish, even going so far as combining the two. Did you know that?*

Yeah. When you're around forever, you kind of figure things out. I thought the fae were tiny little things that irritate the shit out of you all the time about eating right and shit. Like the faeries do. She asked her if she had a faerie. *I did. A long time ago. He was killed when we were at war for some kingdom. After the way he was killed, no one wanted to come around anymore. At one time, it was thought that killing the faerie that was with someone would kill them as well. It didn't work out so well for them.*

No, I would think not. Winnie told her she'd be at the jail to post her bond. *No worries for that. I don't want to be beholden to you. I'll just hang out there until they get their heads out of their asses, and I'll be on my way. After today, I think I've worn out my welcome.*

The police asked her what had happened, and she told them, even going so far as to show them her badge, that she had to get into the place. After telling them what she knew about the men, which was nothing, Imp ended up telling them three more times before someone decided she might need medical care. Not that it mattered. Once the bullet was removed, she'd mend on her own. But she knew better than to just hop right up. She'd have to fake it for a few days at least.

The hospital was state of the art. Imp could also tell it was new, even to the people working in the emergency room. She was given a workup, blood pressure taken, temp too, at least four times so far. The officer with her was too busy flirting with one of the staff to notice she wasn't handcuffed to the bed as they'd told her she'd be.

Not that she had any intentions of leaving. Imp had figured out that what Winnie had told her was true. She was guilty until proven otherwise. Not that it didn't happen a great deal with humans. People just didn't trust as much as they used to.

Smiling to herself, she looked up when her name was spoken. "You must be Winnie Manning." She nodded at her and came fully into the room. There was a man with her, and she introduced him as Hudson, her husband. "You must be a hell of a man to have to put up with Winnie, I'm thinking. She's been a pain in my ass since she convinced me that killing four men would be no trouble for me. But I do know what I am now, so that's all right too, I guess. Why are you here?"

"I'm your attorney." Imp didn't bother pointing out that she didn't need one—she could well represent herself in anything like a courtroom. "Also, the king of dragons would like to meet you. My brother, Cooper. He wants to thank you for making sure one of his people wasn't killed."

"Debra." Hudson nodded. "She's not a dragon. I think I would have smelled brimstone on her had she been one."

"She's the daughter of one of the people that work in his nephew's household. He's very grateful to you." Imp looked at Winnie when she sat down. "You've done a great service for him, and he wishes to grant you anything you wish. Within reason."

"Death." Hudson looked at Winnie when she laughed. "I don't think my wanting to die is all that difficult for him to do, if he's the king of dragons or some shit like that. Just burn me up or something like that, and I'll be happy. You did say he wanted to reward me, correct?"

"Not by death." He looked at his wife. "How did you know that was what she'd ask for? You read her mind, didn't you?"

"No. But I've been where she is. Being around forever. Not having anyone around that you can trust. Yeah, I knew that would be something she wanted." Winnie looked at her. "It wouldn't work anyway, even if Cooper did want to do it for you. You're an immortal, just like us. And I think killing you would be a shame since I do think you're the last of your kind."

"Nope, wrong there. I bet you think you're never wrong, but you are in this. I have not just a sister, but a brother too. We don't...what you might call hang out together. Our combined power would be too much for humans to not feel." She asked her where they were. "I don't know where Glacier is, but my brother is in a cave in Yellowstone. He's been there for decades, keeping away from humans. His name is Ignis." Winnie asked her what her given name was. "Imperium. Imp for short."

The meaning of their names hit Hudson first. When he stood up and sat back down, she watched Winnie. Suddenly the room was filled with faeries and brownies. The order was given to make sure that nothing happened to her.

"I'm guessing you understand what we are. Glacier is ice, Ignis fire. And me the power. But you're wasting your time in protecting me. As you pointed out, I'm an immortal the same as you are." Winnie told her what she was having the little people do. "Ah, so you really know what I am then. What am I? You said you'd tell me."

"You're the power that created dragons' breath. And in turn, created the dragons themselves. Christ, you're everything that...wait until I tell my brother.

He's going to have a shitfit that we didn't figure this out sooner."

When the two of them left her, she looked at the faerie that landed on her belly. She told her what she was called.

"Well, Jasmine, I'm Imp. Are you in charge of the little people?" She said she was hers to command. "I'm not really into the commanding thing. If I ask you for something and you're in the middle of something else, then you tell me that. I don't want you to be taken away from your regular duties while keeping an eye on me so that I don't run."

"No, my lady. I am your faerie forever. I will do as you wish when you wish it." Imp told her she didn't want a faerie. "You must have one. If you are not happy with me as your faerie, there are many more that would gladly take the job."

"It's not that. I don't want anyone to get killed while protecting me, or whatever it is you're thinking I might need from you." She said she'd be fine, that with her, she was an immortal as well.

She'd take it up with someone when she was out of there. She no more wanted a faerie than she did people hanging around with her. Imp had a feeling that once she was out of there, Winnie was going to be up her ass for the rest of her life. Christ, Imp thought, she needed a drink.

~*~

This wasn't the way he wanted to spend his day. Milo knew it was important, but the thought of seeing Jamie's parents just pissed him off. Not that he and Jamie could have been killed, but the way they'd have suffered would have been horrific. Being in the ocean for however long it took someone to find them would have been nothing he wanted to experience.

He looked over at Jamie when she came into the room with him and his parents.

"Are you ready?" Jamie put her hand on her belly and nodded at his mom. "We can do this later if you wish. I'd rather it was finished now, but we can wait if you'd like."

"No. I want this done today. They've had all the time they needed to get this shit going. I'm going to make sure they understand they've fucked with the wrong person." Mom smiled at him. "Do you think this is wrong to go in with this sort of attitude?"

Mom shook her head as she answered Jamie. "No. I was just thinking about how wonderful it is that they're going to be surprised by you not just being alive, but also the fact that you're so pissed off there will be no doubt they'll be able to feel it." Jamie said she hoped so. "I think they're going to be surprised by your power as well. I think you are stronger for it."

"Thanks. Okay, summon them or whatever you have to do." Jamie hugged his mom. "By the way, I'm going to have a baby."

Mom was in mid-summoning when she looked at him. When he nodded, Mom completely forgot what she'd been doing and hugged Jamie. Then she hugged him twice before getting herself ready.

"Patrick Darkhouse and Marie Darkhouse, I summon you to me as the Death Watcher."

They were in mid-argument when they were suddenly in the room. Milo wanted to laugh when Marie's hand connected with Patrick's cheek. Then they both turned to his mom. Dad stood up when Patrick advanced to her, and he suddenly backed off. Milo wondered if he realized he was dead and had just threatened Cindi.

"Hello Mother, Father. What have you been up to?" They both turned to her and looked as shocked as he had hoped they would. "You tried to have me killed. But that's not what I find the most disgusting about you. You also tried to have my sister killed. What were you going to do? Have a big happy reunion with us? Or did you care if I was joining in on the party? Very mean of you, don't you think?"

"I don't have any idea what you're talking about."

Mom told Marie not to lie. When she turned back to Jamie, Marie looked like she was trying her best not to tell the truth. "Tell her your plans."

The compulsion was as strong as he'd ever felt from his mom when she was working with the dead. Sometimes she'd use it to get her point across, but right now, it had the desired effect. Marie started talking at the same time Patrick did.

"You were nothing more than just a pain in the butt to us. Always wanting attention for this or that. Why do children have to be so flipping needy all the time? Then your sister came along, and there was no end to the crap she needed." Patrick said it was the same stuff but triple for Missy. "You have no idea how many times I'd try and drown her when she was tiny, and you'd come into the room screaming at me. I was thrilled to death when she was in that home for kids. It was a wonderful feeling to have the house all to ourselves again."

"You told me you were taking care of her. Then I found out that not only did you put her in that nursing home she's been living in, but you also made sure her insurance would run out, and the state or me would have to pay for her welfare. You did that on purpose." Patrick said it had worked too. "How could you do that to her? Put her in the cheapest care facility you could find, then leave her there without money?"

"It was easy, really. Had we known we were going to die early, we might well have done it sooner. Or not died at all. That was the plan, you see. We had it all set up to be changed into something forever and outlive you. Then some jackass T-boned us, and we were both killed in a stupid accident." Patrick looked at Milo. "How do you like being saddled with Jamie? She's nothing much to look at. Not like her mother, but she'll pass. I'm assuming since the two of you aren't married, you'll be having her out on her butt in no time. Serves her right if you ask me."

"Since you know we were on our honeymoon when you tried to have us killed, I'm going to assume that you're either stupider than I thought, or you have a way to work around my mom's compulsion, to tell the truth." He just smiled at her. "Jamie is going to have a child too. As soon as early next year. What do you think of that? I'll tell you one thing. I'm so happy you're both dead and out of our hair. I'd never allow you to see them even if you were alive and kicking."

"Good. I want nothing to do with them either. Christ, why people want to have children is beyond me." Jamie asked her father why he'd had any. "Your grandmother made us. She said if we didn't have any brats, she'd not leave us anything in her will. I hope she rots in her grave when she's dead."

"I found her. Grandma is coming here to live with us as soon as I can make the arrangements. She's thrilled to know you're both dead too. Especially after you told her that both me and Missy had died." Milo knew she was coming to live with them. It was one of the many things that had upset Jamie so much, knowing that all this time, her grandma had thought them dead. "But that's neither here nor there. As the

Death Slayer, I hereby sentence you to be nevermore. You'll not have any chance of seeing anyone that should die after this day. Your name will be stricken from the books of the dead. Your markers will be magically enhanced so that any ghosts that come across your headstone will know that—"

"Hold on a minute here. What do you mean, Death Slayer? That's the most ridiculous thing I've ever heard. You've made that up to make yourself look better in your in-law's eyes, haven't you?" Marie looked at his mom. "She's always been like this. Making herself out to be a great deal more than she could ever be."

"She's a great deal more than any of us could have hoped for in a daughter-in-law." Dad stood up as he continued. "Your lives will never be brought up again. Not in this world or the next. No one will mourn your passing either. You will be destroyed this day."

Milo reached up his hand, not having any idea why he needed to do so. When his hand filled with a blue sword, gems covered the pummel from tip to tip. He felt the power of it race over his body as he held it upright.

"I, Jamie Manning, hereby destroy you both, Marie Darkhouse and Patrick Darkhouse, from this world and the one beyond." The blade sliced through the air. If it hit them, Milo never felt the hesitation in the swing. "You are no longer a spectrum in either world."

Once they were gone, their screams being cut off immediately, the little boys from earlier appeared. The defiance and arrogance on their faces told him that they were trouble. Maybe not more than Jamie's parents had been, but at least as bad.

Mom addressed them both, calling them by their full names, as they were only children. "Stanley Fitzpatrick Black. David Earl Black. You have been summoned here by order of the Death Watcher. You will be—"

"This is fucking bullshit. We're just kids, you dumbasses. Why the hell do we have to be dead? I've told you this before, you're to make sure you bring us back, or so help me, when I do find someone, I'm going to make sure I kill you right after I do my aunt. You fucking dumbasses." Mom told Stanley that his mother was dead. "No she's not. She would have come for us."

"She's dead. You were told this before, I believe. I've also explained to you that there will be no bringing you back. Dead is dead. And if you ask me, you're lucky to have made it to be as old as you are now."

He glared at his mom harder, then David started spouting off bullshit about how they were going to come back as bigger and stronger men.

"As Death Slayer, you piece of shit, it's my pleasure to inform you that because of the trouble you've caused on both sides of the worlds you've been to, you're going to be erased forever. You will—"

"Blah, blah, blah. Whatever. I don't know who the hell you think you are, but you can blow that shit out your ass. I'm going home. And when I get there, I'm going to hunt up my dad and ask him why the hell he's not dead too." Milo told him his dad was dating and had a good job that he loved. "Bullshit. He was my father, and I think I'd know if he was capable of moving on after our mother killed herself. That's just bullshit."

"You're a little man with words too big for your britches." He looked at Jamie. "I don't know about you, but I'm ready for this to end with them."

The sword seemed to sing to him, a soft tune that was both comforting and soft. As he swung it around, like the first time, he felt it hesitate only for a second as it cut through them both. The sword came alive in his hand and became a small faerie.

"Master Manning. You have done well today with these deaths. The evilness that I encountered was harsh and full of hatred. The worlds will be better served with all of them out of the world. I will be at your call and that of your wife for the rest of your lives." He asked her if she had a name. "I do not unless you wish to call me something. I would enjoy that, I believe. You are the first of very few that have wielded my weight. I am happy and proud to be at your service." Then she turned to Jamie. "I am sorry for your loss, my lady. I do hope you will not hold it against me that I took their lives. I made it as quick and as painful as I could for them."

Jamie laughed. So did his parents when he laughed as well. Gem, he decided to call his sword, told them they must rest and drink plenty of fluids. That juice would be better, but not necessary. Then she put her hand on Jamie's flat belly.

"A daughter grows here. She is like her parents, a wielder of the sword, as well as magical. She isn't fully a dragon, but she will be able to shift into one because of the love you have for her. And the love of her grandparents." Gem turned to Milo's father. "Lord Manning, you are a good man to your family. Your wife as well. I will grant you one boon, one for the two of you. Let me know what it is that you wish, and it will be yours."

"We only wish for our families to continue to have good health and that the children brought here or born to us will also be healthy and happy."

Nodding, Gem turned to Milo again. "And your wish, my lord and lady?" Jamie said she wished for a way to make sure some way that her sisters, Pem and Rachel, could have a single child of their bodies.

"Done. And you, sir? What is it you would wish

for." He told her. "Those are good wishes, my lord and lady. I think wishing that all your brothers, even the ones not yet with their mates, may have a single child of their bodies is a very good and unselfish thing. It is easy to grant those for them."

When she disappeared, Mom grabbed him into her arms and held him as she cried. It was more than she could have hoped for, she told him. More than even his brothers would have been able to have gotten any other way.

Chapter 8

George tried not to look at the webpage he was on. Instead, he focused on what was before him, whatever the hell it was. Laughing a little at his inability to keep himself occupied, he looked again at the time left. Forty-seven minutes and twelve seconds.

"What are you doing?" He looked up to see Milo had entered the room at some point. "You're very distracted. I asked you if you had the pictures that were on the table last night when I left."

"I'm bidding on something." He looked at the time left, the only thing he could see of the auction. "There are still forty-six minutes left. Christ, I think my timer is broken."

"What are you bidding on?" Milo sat down but looked distracted too. "I came here to work out an issue I'm having with my story so far. Maybe you can distract me enough that I can figure it out on my own."

"It's a bunch of teapots. Six of them, as a matter of fact. They're very ugly if you only bought them for their beauty. But one of them is calling to me." Milo asked him what it was saying. He knew his brother, this one anyway, would understand what he was saying. "It's telling me I need to purchase it at any cost. Believe it or not, it then told me to be reasonable about it."

Milo came around to his side of the desk, asking for a view of them. Not wanting to know if he was winning or not, George pulled up the catalog to show them to him. Milo looked at the three pictures that were showing what was in the set.

"They're pretty ugly, George. Do you suppose it is something that just wants to be in a forever home?" George told him it would be if he paid his top dollar for it. "What is your top dollar for it? Since they're listed as a single item, I'm assuming whatever you pay will be times one?"

"No, six. They make that very clear in the description. My highest bid is fifty thousand. That seemed reasonable to me." Milo whistled. "I know. It's not reasonable at all, is it? I just need to see what it wants from me."

Again, Milo seemed to understand what he was saying. Glancing at the clock again, he would see that he'd used up ten minutes of his time. He told Milo how much time was left.

"Can I stay with you while it's going on? I won't tell anyone about the price you have on it, but what's the starting point for them?" He told him. "Okay, so best case scenario is that you pay sixty cents for them. Worst case, you pay fifty grand. How much time is left now?"

"Twenty-nine minutes." This was better. He should have asked Milo to come and keep him sane sooner. "I was looking through some of the catalogs I have for other auctions that are supposed to be for an old estate. The contents on this estate auction are supposed to have been around for seven generations. I wouldn't have any idea about it, but the teapot asked me to come and bid on it. The other things, like a couple of large pieces from the Ming Dynasty, are in the collection as well. Teapots, even uglier ones than this one, go for big bucks online."

They talked about the food pantry, the one he was working on. "I went to a few of the businesses and started this contest for canned goods. The business that gets the most gets a dinner out for all their employees. Mom said not to make it pizza, but something along those lines. Dad said to make it a gift card with an amount on it. That way, they could decide on what it was they want to have for their meal." He laughed a little. "The bank in town has only eight employees, and the insurance company had fifteen. But I bet the bank will win simply because they'll be the underdog in this."

"I like that idea. Did you say what sort of canned goods we wanted? I mean, even boxed food like mac and cheese would be enough to fill a few bellies." Milo said he'd revise it to include boxed things as well. "Also, tell them that they can have the public help them along by picking their favorite place to have people bring by something for the box. That would get the people on the streets involved as well."

Milo made notes, and George looked at the timer. He sighed heavily and looked at his brother, telling him the bidding for the teapots had ended. Being too scared and excited to look on his own, he asked Milo to have a look for him.

It took a little longer than he wanted for Milo to figure out where the bidding prices were. Before he could get it pulled up, George's phone rang. It was the auction house. Making his brother answer it, he wanted to brain him before he finally hung up.

"What did you agree to? Bank draft for the amount. Mom is going to kill me, isn't she? How much? No, don't tell me. I don't want to know either that I didn't win—" Milo put his hand up, and George shut up. "Just fucking tell me."

"Mr. Daniels asked if we wanted to come by and pick it up. After finding out that it was only a few miles from here, I told him we would. Secondly, he wanted to know if you'd continue being a patron of his auction house. I guess you get a discount on the things you buy from them if you're on their mailing list. I told them you'd do that when we were there." George asked him how much again. "Less than we thought at thirty—"

"Mom is going to kill me. I just hope I can appease her by the pot being worth some bucks. Or it tells me where I can take it to be sold to someone stupider than I am." Milo laughed. "I don't find this the least bit funny, Milo. I'm going to tell your wife you hit me. She loves me."

"She loves me more. And I get to sleep with her." Milo smiled. "I didn't say thirty grand, you moron. I was going to say thirty cents. You got them all for thirty cents because you're going to become a patron of the place. The first time you use your new status, you can take fifty percent off items of less than a hundred dollars. So you got— Are you all right, George?"

"Are you fucking kidding me right now? Thirty fucking cents? That's all I paid for them?" Milo said he'd not paid for them yet, but when they went to get them, then he could— George cut his brother off. Again. "You fucking dick. If this is just a joke on your part, I'm not going to be responsible for what I do to you. It's all on you."

"Pull up your email. They said they were sending you the invoice right away." He was shaking so badly he had to put his password in three times before he got it to work. "Just breathe, George, before Winnie shows up and hurts me because you're hyperventilating."

Taking a calm breath in and out, he nodded. Then he put in his password and waited for the connection. As soon as he was able to open his email, the invoice was there. He'd gotten them for less than a buck even with premium price added in, as well as taxes.

"I don't believe this." Milo asked him if he was ready to go. "To pick them up? Of course. Just let me—you know what, we'll go now. I was going to tell Mable that I was going out for a while, but I'll just call her when we get on the road. Because you kept me from being insane, I'll buy you dinner."

"Deal. Pem and Jamie were called into the hospital to perform surgery on a kid that *fell out of a tree.* Neither one of them are buying that just so you know. But his leg is broken in two places, and his arm has been shattered. Jamie told me it looked like he'd been hit with a hammer a couple of times." He asked who it was. "I don't know. She doesn't ask, so I don't know until she finds out for me. But we're going to be paying a visit to someone as soon as we find out. No one needs to beat up on a ten year old. Not like this."

They were on the highway in ten minutes. He's forgotten to print off his invoice, but since he had it on his phone, George thought it would be all right. Even if it wasn't, he was going to take them home, even if he had to steal them away. Laughing, he told Milo what he'd been thinking.

"You do that, and I'm not going to protect you. You do realize that Mom and Dad are both living here now. They won't care how old you are. Mom will make you feel terrible, and Dad will give you that look." George asked him what look. "You know it. The one where he's thinking that he needs to blame himself for your downfall. That he'd raised you better than that, and he's simply a failure. You've seen it. I know I have."

"I remember it now. Sort of a cross between a basset hound and a sad sack." They both laughed, then both of them looked around in the event one of their parents had heard them. "Milo, I have to tell you. All Mom or Dad have to do is say my name in that way they do, and I'm scrambling to find a solution to whatever it is I've done, without any thought to be being nearly three hundred years old. As well as a grown assed man."

"Me too. I don't know where needing to feel sorry came from either. It's like we're ingrained with it from birth or something." They were both still laughing as they pulled into the parking lot. "Are you all right? I'm going to go in with you to look around. I might get rid of some of the shit I've accumulated over the years. A lot of it is just furniture I bought old in the first place. So it'll be ancient by now."

"That's a great idea. I've been paying on several storage lockers since — well, I don't know how long. But keeping it on the off chance it may come back in style is stupid. Maybe I can use the money to get some things I really want. Not that I can think of what that would be right off the top of my head, but I could put it aside."

They were shown to a large room and asked to have a seat less than thirty minutes after George won the bid. They didn't know what was going on, but George didn't like this, so he checked into the mind of the man who had spoken to him last week. When he came into the room, George decided to wait to be told rather than accuse them of some kind of under dealing when it came to his pots.

"We've had two of your teapots stolen, Mr. Manning." George had known this, of course, but hearing it coming out of his mouth was altogether different. "We, of course, are devastated at the loss and will make it up to you in any way you see fit."

"Can he see which teapots are left?" The man was falling all over himself to tell Milo that would be just wonderful. If he said "wonderful" once more, George was going to hit him in the mouth. As soon as the man was out the door, Milo turned to him. "They might not have taken the one you want. However, I'd make sure he knows how disappointed you are. This isn't any way to run a business. It's only been about a half-hour. I have to think it was an inside job."

"You're more than likely right on that. Someone just waiting on the off chance they could get them without paying for them. But why?" Milo shrugged. "I'm too upset to look. You do it before I rape the mind of every person in here." Milo nodded to him as soon as Mr. Deaver came back into the room. His pot was still there, and it was all he could do not to take it and run. "Are you doing an investigation into this?"

"He doesn't need to, George. He's the one that took it. Mr. Deaver here is responsible for a lot of other theft in this place. Mostly it's on groupings like the one you purchased, and he'll help himself to one or two of the pieces and say they were stolen. When in actuality, they're in his office right now, sitting on his desk. Aren't they, Phillip?" Phillip started to back out of the room, and when he was at the doorway, Winnie was there to capture him. "These men are here to arrest him. The rest of his stash of stolen items is in his home. George paid for two more teapots that are in the office here."

"Thanks, guys. I've been having reports run across my desk since I've been here. I had no idea it was anything more than just petty theft. This takes it to a whole new level with there being so many other things taken." Winnie smiled at them both. "I love this gig, by the way. Helping out the police department for a little while."

Deaver was read his rights and taken away. Right out the front door where everyone could see him being arrested.

Winnie was watching the police department while the man in charge of the place was on a two-week vacation. George thought she was having a good deal more fun than she should have been, but it was working out. George had a feeling that if the man didn't return, his aunt would do the job for free. She was having so much fun.

"I think she's enjoying this so much. She might live here too." George thought the same thing. "What do you think she thinks is fun about it?"

"I don't know. Also, I'm not sure others would think what she's doing is called *fun*. I think crime is down by a great deal, not that there was much here anyway. And there have been fewer fights at the bars nightly." Milo said that was what she was more than likely enjoying. The feel of accomplishment. "I think you might be right. Not many dragons are fucking up nowadays, and people, for the most part, still don't believe in them. Maybe she's just bored."

"Could be." An officer brought him in the final two teapots. Them being in person didn't improve their looks at all. George thought they might be uglier now that he could see them. "Christ, what was I thinking?"

Open me. George looked at Milo and asked him if he'd heard it too. When he nodded, both of them sat down with the teapot between them. *Take off this stuff so I can breathe again, Young George. I need my air.*

The outside of the pot was polymer clay that had been baked at a very low temperature to make it seem harder than it really was. Carefully pulling the chunks away from the teapot, George could see that it was jade. Very old and very dark jade.

"George?" He sat back and looked at the piece when ninety percent of the clay was pulled free. "That's a dragon. I don't know if you can tell or not, but that looks like our grandma. Our Dad's mother. Weren't we told she was a jade-colored dragon?"

~*~

No one touched the teapot. It was beautifully done, Jamie thought. The way someone had etched the dragon into the entire pot, using her tail for the handle and her mouth for the spout, made her think whoever had done this had seen an actual dragon. Even the clawed feet that made up the pot's footer was as realistic as anything she'd ever seen. Jamie had even nicked her finger on one of the claws that curved up and down on it.

The detail was exquisite. The colors of the

carved areas were done in such a way it enhanced the three-dimensional dragon rather than take away from it. The writing on it, something that she had no idea how to read, was carved in the greatest detail she'd ever witnessed.

"I love the attention to detail on all of it. But the fact that they carved the dragon, so it looks more like it's resting on the teapot rather than a part of it, is what makes me think someone knew what they were doing in hiding it. The gold tips of the scales makes her look like she's resting after a long flight." Jamie had to agree. The sole reason for hiding it in plain sight had to be very telling. She asked Xavier if it was true, that it was his mother. "I don't know for certain. I will tell you I've not thought of my mom as much as I used to. It's been longer than I care to think on at times. I was the youngest of the six, so I don't have as many memories as the others do. But I do remember my uncle telling me once that there was a human that did carvings and that my mom had been asked to sit for him. I don't know what it was she sat for, but I'm reasonably sure this could be her."

The top of the lid had a broken egg, decorated with not just diamonds but emeralds as well. The gold used carefully had been used as highlights. The circle around the egg was where they found the smallest dragon just outside the broken shell of its birth. The tiniest slivers of emeralds in the larger dragon's eyes seemed to be able to follow a person around the room. Winnie had even unearthed six equally beautiful teacups from the stash of Deaver that had golden rings around the cup's rim to sit it level on any surface. No handles were on the cups, and it took her a few moments to realize they'd not been broken off but had never been on it.

Asking and being told that she could pick it up, she was surprised at how light it was. Not paperweight light, but not nearly as heavy as she had assumed it would be. Putting it back on the table, she asked George if he'd had any more conversations with it.

"Not yet. It told me it was finally free to breathe and that she'd talk to me later, but nothing more than that. How much do you think it's really worth? Not that it matters—I'm just glad to have it." George laughed a little. "You don't seem surprised that I can talk to things."

"Did Uncle Cooper say when he was coming by to see it? I mean, he's the oldest. Maybe he has some insight on it." Milo asked what he'd missed. "Oh, I told Jamie about your ability when we were talking one night."

"He said he was on his way. That's all he said." George sat across from Milo as he continued. "You have no idea how much I want to make a cup of tea in this thing. Just to see it pour into one of the cups. And then taste it. I don't know what I'm expecting it to taste like, but I'm hoping it'll be as close to what this thing looks like in magnificence."

"Why don't you? I mean, it's a teapot, right? You should do it." George told Jamie he wanted Cooper to see it first. That way, if it was his mom, he thought all of the brothers should have the first pot. Jamie was visibly impressed as she told George that. "Wow, that's really sweet of you, George. Who would have thought you were a romantic like that?"

"Don't get used to it. I'm trying to get brownie points to use later. Having an uncle king of your kind surely does put a damper on your life at times." They were laughing when the front door was opened. As soon as they realized it was Cooper and Carson, each of them stood up. Even Jamie did. "Uncle Cooper, I found something today. Well, three weeks ago, but I didn't get it until today. I wasn't going to—" Someone cleared their throat. "I'm sorry. I'm just really nervous. Did your mom really pose for a man that did jade carvings? That's important to know."

"Yes. I don't remember the man's name, but yes, she did it. In exchange for her sitting for him, she was able to take as many sheep as she wished, so long as she didn't take them all, to feed us boys with. I think there were times when that was all there was between us starving or not. Why do you ask?" George moved out of the way, and Cooper looked around the room before looking at the teapot. "Holy shit, George. Holy shit. It's Mom. I'd know that carving anywhere. He brought it to the cave we were living in and showed it to us. It was so tiny to us then, nothing more than a speck in his palm. But that's it."

Cooper asked if he could touch it. "Yes, of course. I don't know what the writing says at the bottom of it, but the cups were found by Aunt Winnie. She found them when someone tried to steal them —" He caught himself again. "It spoke to me. From the catalog. It begged me to pay any price to purchase it. Then it went silent other than to ask me to remove the polymer clay that was baked around it to hide it, I guess."

"It says here...." Cooper had to sit down, and he held the teapot to his heart. "It says *To my favorite dragon. I have named her Ava.* That was my mother's name from then on. Ava." He wiped at the tears, and Jamie could feel her own eyes filling with unshed emotions. "Have you told the others yet? What did Xavier say about it?"

"He didn't know." Cooper turned to his younger brother and asked him about it. He said the same thing to his elder brother as he had to them. He just didn't remember her. George continued. "I was just telling Jamie here that you and the others should be the ones that use it first. I want you to tell me in great detail how it tastes, too."

They were laughing as Winnie and Hudson,

now that he was there, gathered up the other uncles. Like Cooper, they were moved to tears at the sight of the little teapot, and Jamie had to go and get boxes of tissues for the family.

Jamie had learned to make tea the Chinese way when she'd been in college. One of her roommates had been from a very traditional family, and she'd learned from her great grandmother. She did that now to show them she had as much knowledge of the jade teapot as they did. Not their mother, of course, but of the pouring tea ritual.

When the tea was ready, she told Cooper, as head of the household back when it was just the six of them, and waited while he sipped the tea, holding the tiny looking cup in his big strong hands. He sat his cup down, having only taken a sip. Cooper burst into tears as soon as his brothers did the same with his cup.

"I'll pay you ten times what you paid for it, George. I won't take no for an answer, either. I would love to be able to pull this out when I need a pick me up, and share it with my family. On special occasions, of course. Ten times what you paid is a lot of money." Milo laughed so hard it was difficult not to join him. "Have I missed something?"

"Ten times is a very reasonable amount, George. If nothing else, you should be happy he's not making you hand it over." Cooper said he'd not do that for any amount of money. Their uncle Lincoln said he was trying to make a point. That made Milo and George laugh all the harder. "I don't see what is so funny."

"You can have it for ten times what I paid for it, Uncle Cooper." George, still fighting laughter, handed his uncle the bill of sale. "With the six teapots I got, that comes to five cents each. So you owe me fifty cents. I don't know how much the cups were—they were brought here by Winnie when she found the other things in the man's office—but they're yours anyway. For the price of telling me how the tea tasted."

They were all laughing then, and Cooper asked her if she'd make more tea for the others. She was glad now that she'd paid attention to her friend and remembered that rushing a good cup of tea was the same as rushing through a shitty job at painting. The art of it was lost.

They all had a cup of the delicious brew. Cooper didn't sip the second time but stared into the cup. Jamie asked him if he could read tea leaves.

He smiled at her. "I can, but I don't know how good at it I am. The last time I did it was when I was just a young dragon. The man who carved this gave each of us a cup and then read our leaves. Mine said that I was destined for great things. All my mind could think of was being like my father, king of all dragons.

I guess it came true." He dumped his leaves onto the surface of the table after drinking the tea and stared down at them. "It says I'm going to live a long and very fruitful life. That usually means children. That I'll have enough good fortune that I will forever have a spark to light the fire and enough sense to get in out of the rain." He looked at it harder. "I'm sorry, I read it wrong. It says I'll have enough sense to know that water is the root of both evil and good. That's about right, I think."

They took turns having their leaves read by Cooper. He enjoyed it as much as the rest of them did. When it was time for supper, Cooper and Carson took them all out. Telling them not to get used to him being such a generous man, he hugged George to him.

"This is far and away the best thing that someone has given me and the rest of my brothers, George. I don't know what to say about how you've made me feel." George told him it would be his pleasure for him to just take it. That giving it to him had been his plan all along. "Thank you. I'll make it up to you."

"Before I forget." Jamie stood next to Milo as he looked at his uncle. "I've been given a new job, as I'm sure you know from my mom. But she asked me to make sure I let you know what I've…what Jamie and I have done for this family. The ability to have children that aren't dragons, but will have some of their traits, is now there for any of us second generation to have."

No one moved. They did look at Milo like he had a second head or something. Finally, it was Xavier that stood up and thanked them. Then it was a free for all on all of them hugging the two of them. It was Finn that thanked him the most.

"A child of her own? You've no idea how much she's been wanting one. Rachel has never said anything, but I can feel her sadness every night when she's supposed to be sleeping. I don't know what you did to make this happen, Milo and Jamie, but I owe you everything right now. There isn't a thing I'd not do for you or even pay you for the happiness I feel right now." Milo told them what they'd done and how Gem had told them what a wonderful job they'd done for her and her kind. "This is wonderful. You've no... well, I guess you do have an idea. That's wonderful."

"Also, we're going to have a child too. A daughter."

More cheers went up, and there was much hugging from everyone. Even though Xavier and Cindi knew, they acted like they were given the news for the first time ever. Jamie certainly did love this family and their ways of making a person feel so welcomed and a part of something larger than she'd ever had before.

After everyone left, she and Milo sat on the couch and enjoyed the evening air from the open doors in the living room. She didn't need to have television to watch. No job was pressing her. All she had was her thoughts. Until the little boy and his accident of falling out of the tree returned to her mind.

She turned to tell Milo what she knew and found him sound asleep. Even his face was so relaxed that he had his mouth open, and soft snores mingled with the sound of his heart as it beat in his chest. Jamie realized in that moment that she was indeed in love with Milo Manning and wondered why it had taken her so long to realize he was the most important person in her life. And would be forever.

When she snuggled up to him, he wrapped his arm around her and pulled her closer to his body. In seconds, less she thought, she was beginning to feel her own body relaxing. Soon she knew she'd be as asleep as he was.

Chapter 9

Milo didn't move. His back was hurting from sitting in one position for so long, but the little boy in front of him, lying on the bed, needed his comfort, and he was going to give it to him. Jamie came into the room while he was adjusting his fingers that Caleb was holding onto.

"How's he doing?" Milo, whispering as she had, told her how he'd woken up several times and spoken, but mostly it was about how much pain he was in. "I have given him a little extra in the way of meds up until now. But I need him to wake up so I can talk to him. Winnie does as well. All we have him listed as being a victim of right now is neglect. I'm sure you know as well as I do that it's much more than that."

"I do. I can't read his mind right now. His pain

is blocking out everything else. I do know that both his parents were in on this falling out of the tree shit." She said that Winnie had told her the same thing. "He's been holding my hand since he woke up the first time. He said it was making him feel like he could depend on me to make sure he was all right. Nothing about his parents, however. Not even to ask where they were. Where are they, by the way?"

"Daniel Merchant is sitting in jail right now for neglect by way of not bringing him in when he first fell, or whatever. Winnie is looking for his wife, Mary." Milo asked her what she thought about what they'd talked about before. "Adopting him? Yes. I want to do it if this goes south the way I think it should. I guess your parents are going to be in sometime today to talk to him. Nothing earth-shattering, but just to talk to him about his life up until now."

"I don't think it's been all that good, do you?" She told him what she'd found when they did the X-rays when he'd been brought in. "So he's been beaten on a regular basis. Poor fella. My heart just breaks for him."

They both looked at Caleb when he moaned. Milo could see that his face was registering all sorts of pain. But when he smiled at him, Milo was sure he could take on the world and come out the winner.

"How are you, buddy? My wife is here. Do you remember her?" Caleb turned his head slowly and started to close his eyes. "Caleb, we need you to wake up a little more. All right? Just so we can talk to you a little while."

"I hurt." Jamie took his other hand and told Caleb she was sorry. "My arm hurts really bad, Doctor. Do you think I could have something for it? Not a lot. Maybe a baby aspirin or something? I hurt a lot."

"I know you do, Caleb, but I need to talk to you. Then you can have something for the pain. I think I can give you a little more than some baby stuff too." He looked at Jamie, but he didn't cry again as he had before. "I need to talk to you about what we had to do to fix up your arm. Can you remember how you hurt it?"

Dangerous ground, but when Winnie just appeared in the room where Caleb couldn't see her, Milo felt better. They'd been warned several times that his room was being recorded, as all the new rooms were, and not to put words in his mouth. Such as asking if his parents had been lying when they said he'd fallen from a tree.

"Momma did it with Dad. They said if I was hurt really bad, they'd not have to get up early in the morning to take me to school. I don't understand that. I got no school in the summer. Can I have a drink, please? My mouth is powerful dry. It can just be some spit in a glass if that's what you got."

Milo looked at Jamie when he asked for spit to drink. She asked him if he drank other people's spit a great deal. His nod, then his verbal reply, made Milo's skin crawl. Christ, the things this kid was having to endure was enough to make him want to throw up.

"I can get you some ice chips to chew on. Would that help?" Caleb looked at Jamie with one eye as if he didn't believe his luck. Nodding again, Milo put out his other hand, and a glass of ice chips appeared in his hand, which he handed to Jamie. None of them wanted him to go without ever again.

As she was putting the chips in his mouth, Milo noticed that Jamie's hands were shaking. Taking the spoon and glass from her, he watched as she sat back down and cried a little. His heart broke for her as well. To think that as a surgeon, she had to go through this with a child.

"Caleb, can you tell me why you asked for spit?" He told her, and Milo knew that for as long as he lived, he'd never forget the look of pure anger on Jamie's face right then. "Instead of giving you a glass of water or even an ice cube, your parents would spit in a cup for you to drink? I'm sorry you had to do that."

"It's all right. It's better than when they pee in a glass for me. It's not good tasting, and it's hot too. Can I have some ice, please?"

Milo filled the spoon and started for his mouth.

Winnie grabbed his hand to still it. Milo could see how many chips were on the spoon and had he put them in his mouth at the rate of speed in which he was aiming at an unseen face, he would have hurt the boy. Winnie took both items away from him and put the chips in his mouth herself.

Neither he nor Jamie were fit to ask the little boy anything. He was tiny too. His twelve year old body was that of a much younger child, underdeveloped and underfed. Milo wondered how he'd survived the treatment he'd been having done to him.

"Caleb, your dad told us that you fell from the tree. Is that what happened?" Milo watched as Winnie, this time, put questions to Caleb. Her hands were steady and her voice calm, neither of which he would have been able to do under the circumstances. Caleb looked at him before saying anything.

Jamie spoke then. "I have to be sure there are no other broken bones in your body, Caleb. Falling from a tree and hurting your arm the way you did, I would think you would have been at a very high point in the tree." Jamie glanced at him. "You have a lot of other places that are broken in your ribs and your arms and legs, but they're old breaks that it seems to me, as a doctor, no one cared for."

"Go ahead, Caleb. Tell my wife. She is a good doctor and only wants the best for you. So do I. You told me you trusted me. Is that still true?" He nodded, still looking as terrified as he had when he'd turned to him. "I swear to you, Caleb, nothing will ever hurt you again so long as I'm alive. And I'm going to live forever."

"You promise?" Milo was almost ready to tell him to forget it. His voice, low and full of fear, scared him a great deal. "They said I'd be put in the well again. I don't like it down there. There are bones and stuff. Then when they pulled me out, I'd be taken to a home for bad kids. It might be better than I have now, but I'm not a bad boy."

"No, you're not." Milo looked up at Winnie when she said his name. When she mouthed what to ask him next, Milo cleared his throat to continue. Jamie left them there. He could almost taste her anger and pain. "You said the well had bones in it. I'm not sure what you mean. Doesn't it have water in it? I mean, that's what I'd think."

When Caleb leaned closer, he did too. "It's my grandma and my sister. They didn't do what they were told. The baby bones are not as scary as my grandma's—she really loved me. That's why they took her away from me." He had to ask, and it was on the tip of his tongue to do so, but Caleb continued before he could. "They told her she was being too nice to me and that it was my fault she had to go in the well. My sister, she fell in when she was looking at Grandma. But I think my mom pushed her in."

Milo asked about the baby bones. "Mom did that. She said it wasn't breathing when she had it, so she thought it'd be cheaper to just put her in there with my grandma rather than have to pay for a funeral. I didn't say anything. I know I should have, but I was afraid of being in there too. You understand, don't you, Mr. Milo?"

"Yes. I'm glad you didn't join your sisters and grandma in the well." He told him that the baby was a little boy. "So you had a sister and a little brother too?"

"Yes, sir. I wish sometimes I was brave enough that I could go in the well too. But I couldn't do it. Mom said they'd be better off without me sucking them dry, but I didn't go by the well enough so I could fall too." Milo looked at Winnie when she shivered. Milo was glad Caleb couldn't see her right now. She was in full body armor, and her wings were spread out behind her. "I remember that the doctor told me I'd lost my arm. Mom is sure going to be mad when I can't do the laundry and stuff."

"You can do anything you did before. You'll just have to figure out how to modify your ways of doing something. You don't have to ever think of yourself as anything but a good kid who got a bum deal out of life. But you're going to persevere. All right?" Caleb nodded but didn't look convinced. "Caleb, would you like to come and stay with us until things get settled?"

"Yes. I'd do all the work you want me to without complaining, too. I promise." Milo was so choked up he could do nothing more than nod. "If you ever have a baby, Mr. Milo, I'll go away and not bother any of you again if you don't want me anymore. I swear it. I know kids can be draining. That's what my momma told me."

"We are going to have a baby, Caleb. However, when she's born, if you're still living with us, you'll be her big brother. There will be no laundry that you have to do, although I think everyone should know how to separate clothes and wash and dry them. You never know when you might need that skill. Cooking too. That could—" Winnie cleared her throat. She looked better, too, just plain Winnie. He looked back at Caleb. "I'm going on about stuff. You have no idea how excited we are to take you home with us. And if Officer Winnie here can make things work out, we might be able to keep you for the rest of your life."

"You'll be nice to me. I know it." Milo told him he could count on it. "Thank you, Mr. Milo. I hope you mean that my momma and dad will be in jail, where I think they belong. They killed my grandma and my little sister."

Milo held Caleb while he sobbed. Each time he did that little hiccup thing, it tore at his heart more. Jamie joined them then, and when she asked if they were all right, Milo realized he was crying too. Jamie handed him a tissue and sat back down. She was in her serious mode now.

"Caleb, I'm so sorry about this, but I have to talk to you about your arm. We tried to save it, but the bone was beyond fixing. Do you understand what I'm telling you? I did speak to you one other time when I was in here, but I don't know that you were able to focus on what I was saying. You were still drugged up." He looked at her but didn't let go of Milo's hand. "I'm so sorry, honey. Whatever happened to you, it was just too much damage for us to be able to save."

"I remember it. Sort of. Mr. Milo said I could do whatever I wanted, only that I'd have to be able to change the way with how I do it." He looked at the bloodied bandage. "It's going to make me not be able to do some things, but he said I could figure it out. Mr. Milo wants me to go and stay with you guys too and said that you're going to have a baby."

"Yes, we are. You're all right with what is wrong with your arm, honey?" He first nodded, then shook his head. "I understand that. But you're very calm, and I want to make sure that if you have any questions, you can ask me about it. I'm here for you, Caleb, and hopefully will be forever, as Milo told you."

He did have questions, a great many of them, but not a one about his arm or the lack of it. Caleb asked about the baby. If they had a pool. Then he asked if the two of them were living in a house. It took him a moment to figure out that he meant a house rather than a box. Luckily, Jamie understood and told him they had a house and that he'd have his own room with his own bathroom, something he'd not had at home—a working bathroom.

"Mr. Milo, I'm really tired. Do you think I could get some water to drink? Doctor Manning said I could have more than an aspirin. I'd like that now." Jamie had been pulled away for another surgery. They were hoping, it seemed, and nothing was even officially open yet. "My stubby hurts. I'm gonna call it that so kids won't be able to call me names."

It took them less than two minutes to bring him a shot of something for pain. Milo could tell it was hitting him hard when Caleb smiled and closed his eyes. Milo went into the hall to find where Winnie had gone. Wherever it was, he was sure it wasn't boding well for someone. Milo hoped it was Caleb's biological parents. It would be good that Winnie got to them before he did. They'd be dead if he did.

~*~

George was walking to the pantry warehouse when he saw the police race by him. While he had no idea what was going on, he hoped it had a lot to do with the Merchants that were connected with Caleb. He was nearly to the place he was headed when his mom joined him as she came out of the store on Main.

"I've been thinking a great deal about you, son." He said whatever it was, he'd not done it. "I'm sure you didn't. Of all my sons, you would confess faster if you had done anything the others would try to hide from me. No, I wanted to talk to you about your home. I'm hearing you don't particularly care for it. Tell me what it is that you don't like. If we can resell it, then we will. But with this family and the way we collect humans, someone will live in it. The family will repay you, George. That's only fair since we picked so badly for both you and Milo."

"I don't know how you found out, Mom, but it's all right that I live there." She told him she wanted him to be happy to live there. "I am. I see no point in dwelling on the things I don't like because maybe, whoever my mate is, she'll not like it either, and we can move to her place. Which will be older and more lovely than the pile of bricks I'm currently dwelling in."

"You said that perfectly, I think. Dwelling, not living. I want to make this right for you." He told her he had it. "I know you have it, George, but what I'm worried about is that it'll make or break your mate if she comes around, and doesn't stick around because of *your pile of bricks,* as you called it. You're still as blunt as ever, aren't you?"

"I love you too, Mom. About the house? I don't like it at all. There are very few redeeming things about it that I can point out and say I do enjoy." She laughed, and he joined her. "Too blunt? I have been told that I'm sometimes too blunt to the point of rudeness."

"You are, but that's all right. I love that quality about you. All right. What is it you'd like in a house? Older style? The reason I asked is because you mentioned that you didn't care for bricks and you liked older homes. I think I might have just the place for you. Come on, I'll take you there."

"Mom, I'm sort of busy." She told him it wouldn't take but a moment, and he found himself in an entrance hall that he immediately fell in love with. "Oh, Mom, this is it. I don't even have to go any further—unless the rest of the house is a shit hole. Please tell me it's as grand looking as this."

The two of them popped in and out of the rooms. As far as he was concerned, it was the perfect home for him. Even the furniture was perfect. He asked her about that.

"The person who lived here for most of her life has passed away. I know that knowing she died in her bed won't bother you. Right?" He said it didn't. "The house is going on the auction block later this afternoon. The furniture as well. I have a good feel for how much people are willing to pay for it. However, I don't think it's nearly enough. The furniture will be something you have to decide on. I would, if I were you, just flat outbid what you're willing to pay for it all and tell them you're willing to take it as is. I'd go at least a hundred and fifty thousand. Minimum."

"How much are people willing to pay?" She told him. "You're right, Mom. Sixty thousand is much too low for this place. Lock stock and barrel, how much should it all go for at the auction today?" Mom said she knew that most people, unlike them, were not into antiques. "So things will go fairly cheap, you're thinking."

"I do. I mean, there are a few pieces that will go higher. That's why if you purchase it with a full price, you'll be in it in no time." He asked her how much would be the cutoff. "I'd say if you were to have to go to even half a million, you'd be doing very well. It will need some updates, but the faeries here would do that for you at no cost to anyone. They actually enjoy working for us."

"Because you guys are dragons." He looked at his watch. "How long do I have? I'm assuming not long, as there are people in the house now taking the furniture out."

"You have two hours. Go talk to the realtor on site right now. I'll go with you." When Mom said she'd go, that didn't mean she was going to take over at any point. She would just be there, standing on the sidelines, waiting for someone to ask her what she thought. "You have my full support."

That he knew.

Finding the realtor took him longer than it should have, he thought. When he did find him, George could see the dollar signs going off in his head. George, always telling it like it was, smiled.

"I can let you take the highest bid you get today, which won't be nearly what I'm going to pay for all of it. Or I'll walk away right now. It doesn't matter if I get this or not. I can find houses for a dime a dozen." The realtor, Jimmy Banks, told him he'd have to talk to the family. Then he asked what he was willing to pay. "You tell them what I want to do, and we'll work from there. Whatever they want isn't going to cut it. I want a fair deal."

"Yes, of course. I'll go and get them now." When he left them, George looked at his mom. She was laughing hard behind her hand, and he leaned over and kissed her on the cheek. The family of the woman that had owned the house looked as eager to sell as he wanted to buy. But neither of them were as cagy as he was. "I've told them what you'd like to do, and they're willing to listen to your proposal."

"How much to end this auction and you walk away?" The man, older than the two women, asked him what his price would be. "My price is dependent on what you want. I'm a buyer, not the seller. I want it as is, all the furniture too. Right now. Or, as I said to him, I'll walk away, and you'll take what you get from the buyers."

"Can we talk about it?"

He nodded, and they walked away. One of the women turned back and looked at him. "You'll take everything as it sits right now? No coming back if the roof is messed up, which it is. Also, the kitchen needs to be updated. My mom, she passed away in this house as well. I have to tell you that anyway, but I thought you might want to know that." The woman just looked at him as if she was waiting for him to say no deal. "Also, you should also know that there isn't any cable in the house, nor Internet. Mom didn't want it in her home."

"I know what is wrong with it. I've looked the house over since we arrived. Also, I want to point out that includes the two lots on either side of the home. As I said, as it sits right now." She nodded, and the three of them walked away. George looked at his mom. "Are they just that honest, or did you have something to do with them telling me the things wrong with it?"

"No, I didn't. But this is the report that Winnie gave me just now that tells everything the inspector has found wrong with the house. She was right in the stuff she told you. But as I said, it's an easy fix for you. Also, I don't know if you noticed this or not, but you're across the street from Jamie and Milo. That's a perk I'd not realized until right now."

Within five minutes of people beginning to

show up around the house, he noticed that the movers taking stuff out of the house had stopped. There were people to bid on things coming around too. George wanted to tell them they were there for nothing, but he didn't want to jinx the deal. The trio came back to stand in front of him and Mom.

"We're willing to let it all go for two hundred grand. I don't think it's worth that much, to be honest with you, but this way, we'll have enough money to share and pay off some of the debt we have from taking care of Mom and Dad. Even though she died here, our dad's medical bills were also outrageous. This will help me be able to pay for a couple of years of college for my kids too." Milo started to tell him it was a deal, but the man spoke again. "If that's too much, we can take a hundred and fifty. I'm sorry about that."

"I tell you what. I'll pay the two hundred grand and find you a good attorney that will make it, so you're not responsible for the debts of your parents." He winked at his mom before continuing. "This is my mom, Cindi Manning. She'll also find a way for your kids to get scholarships for college at no cost to you guys. Do we have a deal?"

The man broke down. Sobbing his thanks out, he held onto George until he finally regained control of himself. Shaking his hand, again and again, he thanked him, as did his wife, as it turned out, and his sister. It was up to the auctioneer to settle up with the people there.

George turned to his mom. "Was that all right with you?" She told him it was perfectly fine. "If there is a problem with their application, tell me. I'll gladly pay for the kids to go to college. It's for a good cause, and I think their parents will make them study hard, don't you?"

"I do."

There were a lot of people yelling about the sale of everything, but the auctioneer and the realtor had it under control. As he and his mom walked into the house, they were greeted by Winnie and a bunch of faeries. By a bunch, George was sure that it was perhaps several thousand of them. They were vibrating to get started on the house.

"George, honey, set them to work before they tear the house down."

He was laughing at his mother when he told them what he was looking for in the way of the kitchen. He stressed several times that they'd have to wait until the people were gone, but he could see that they were very disappointed. George was excited for this new venture. He nearly asked his mom if the push was because his mate was coming but didn't. He wanted to be as surprised as the rest of them when she showed up.

AWARD WINNING, BESTSELLING AUTHOR

Kathi Barton, a winner of the Pinnacle Book Achievement Award and a best-selling author on Amazon and All Romance books, lives in Nashport, Ohio, with her husband, Paul. When not creating new worlds and romance, Kathi and her husband enjoy camping and going to auctions. She can also be seen at county fairs with her husband, who is an artist and potter.

Her muse, a cross between Jimmy Stewart and Hugh Jackman, brings her stories to life for her readers in a way that has them coming back time and again for more. Her favorite genre is paranormal romance, with a great deal of spice. You can visit Kathi online and drop her an email if you'd like. She loves hearing from her fans. aaronskiss@gmail.com.

Follow Kathi on her blog: http://kathisbartonauthor.blogspot.com/

www.ingramcontent.com/pod-product-compliance
Lightning Source LLC
Chambersburg PA
CBHW030223180626
46810CB00008B/2941